Metrofloat New York

William Quincy Belle

A Post-apocalyptic Sci-Fi Thriller

BG Ltd.

Disclaimer

This is a work of fiction. Any names or characters, businesses or places, events or incidents, are fictitious. Any resemblance to actual persons, living or dead, is ... Well, what are the chances?

Prologue

The stars were out. The air was fresh. From the fiftieth-floor terrace, the muted sounds of the city were a dull roar. Willard Bachmann, balding but a commanding presence in his sixty-fourth year, moved along the balustrade, sipping an arti-sour and staring at the vista before him: to the one side, the skyline of one of Earth's largest floating metropolises — Metrofloat New York — and to the other, a kilometer below, vast desert plains ending in the silhouette of a distant mountain range. It was all his. He controlled it. He ruled it.

Years of hard work, important decisions, and backroom dealings had amassed for him an unprecedented amount of power and influence. The OligCouncil was no longer something he could lead — it was something he could commandeer and rule. He could bend it to his will. He could possess it and do with it what he wanted.

This was his opportunity. Instead of going through the never-ending and often useless democratic process of consensus, he could force his will on everyone. There was no campaigning for buy-in. There was no vote for agreement. Everyone had to do as he said. Period. *Dictatorship*: the fast and easy way to get things done. Willard chuckled to himself. The word had such a negative connotation. He would say *enlightened absolutism* or *philosophical monarchism*. He was taking it upon himself to bring people together, to get them to pull in the same direction, and to remove the self-interest and deindividuation plaguing society.

Willard put one hand on the railing and leaned out over the dizzying height. He held up his glass toward the city panorama and said, "To you. Together, we will be great once again." He took the last sip of his drink, turned, and walked across the balcony. Slipping through the open door, he waved his hand over a sensor to close it. Tomorrow would be a busy day; he needed to sleep.

He sauntered across a sizable living area to an open kitchen and set down his glass. As Willard turned toward the bedroom, a movement caught his eye. He looked across the expanse of floor to the windows facing the terrace. The edge of a curtain fluttered. The door leading to the balcony was open — the door he had shut a moment ago.

Willard crept around the kitchen island into the living room. He skirted a decorative shelving unit and moved into the corner, his work area. Opening a drawer of his desk, he removed a pulsed energy pistol. The charge indicator showed eighty percent.

He held the gun up at arm's length and scanned the room for any movement. Nothing. He grasped the handle of a Japanese samurai sword displayed on the wall, slid it out of its case, and moved from behind the desk.

Willard swept the area and looked behind various pieces of furniture. He held his breath and listened. From somewhere came the hum of machinery, electricity, and background noises typical of any building in the city, but nothing else.

To the left, the floor creaked. Willard whirled and fired. There was a thump followed by the crackling of a fireball against the wall. Nothing was there. Willard glanced left and right, waving the gun in preparation for a second shot. His ears became accustomed to the silence and he remained still, listening for breathing, the shuffle of a foot — anything. There was nothing but silence. Was anybody there? The door was open, but he had shut it. He was sure of it. Since this was the fiftieth floor, whoever had come in from the terrace had chosen an unorthodox way of dropping in unannounced.

Willard checked the other half of the room, walking to the far end of the couch and looking behind it. Nothing.

A tiny noise came from his work area in the corner. Turning, he pointed the pistol in that direction, but it was difficult to see in the subdued light. He could feel his heart beating. Someone was here. Someone was waiting for the right moment.

As he stared into the corner, trying to discern any movement, something registered in his peripheral vision. But it was too late. A hand grabbed the gun and twisted forward while another grabbed his forearm and twisted backward. Willard had tensed his finger and the pistol fired at the couch, scorching the fabric.

The gun wrenched from his hand, Willard turned toward his attacker and swung the sword in an arc over his shoulder. The blade hit the attacker's upper arm with a thud and buried itself deep in the limb. There was no blood. Willard's eyes widened as he realized what he had cut into was not human flesh.

The assailant tossed the pistol to one side and seized the blade, pulling upward to remove it from his arm and back to yank the handle out of Willard's hand. He tossed the sword aside, and it jangled against the floor. Willard leaped and kicked the intruder in the stomach, causing the assailant to lose his balance and fall backward. Willard dove for the pistol, twisted around, and took aim. There was no sign of his attacker.

He jumped up and ran back to the couch. Seeing nothing, he spun around, checking all three hundred and sixty degrees around him. His heart raced, his breathing hard. The adrenaline had kicked in, and Willard's hands shook as he tried to steady the gun.

"Mr. Bachmann." The male voice was sonorous.

Willard spun toward the sound and fired. He saw part of the man's head as he ducked behind a bookcase, just before the fireball shattered a crystal vase.

"Mr. Bachmann," the voice said, "you're making this far too difficult."

Willard moved toward the bookshelf, holding the pistol up with both hands.

"You must face the inevitable. We all have our time, and you, sir, have had yours."

Willard crouched down, trying to see between the open shelves.

"This can be painless, or it can be painful."

Willard aimed between two shelves, over the top of a line of books. His hands were shaking, and his aim was off. The charge sputtered against the spines and a wisp of smoke curled up.

He ran to the side of the bookcase and spun around behind it, yet saw no one. Wondering what to do next, Willard heard a step to his right. He fired. The discharge sizzled in the middle of the man's chest and singed his shirt. It did not stop him.

The attacker grabbed Willard's right arm at the wrist, held it over his head, and then seized him by the throat and squeezed.

"Please drop the gun, Mr. Bachmann."

The two men held each other's gaze until Willard let go of the pistol, which fell to the floor with a clatter.

"Thank you." The attacker pushed Willard across the room into a straight-backed chair. He snapped restraining devices in place, locking each wrist to an arm of the chair.

Willard looked at his adversary's arm but could no longer see the cut from the sword. "Auto-regen. I've heard of it but didn't think it had yet been perfected for the market."

"If you know the right people and have the money, anything is possible." The man uncoupled a tubular device from his belt and fiddled with the controls.

"Do I get a cigarette? A last meal? A final request?"

"This won't hurt, Mr. Bachmann. Well, I've been given to understand it doesn't hurt, but does anybody know for sure?"

Willard gave a warped smile. "Nobody who's undergone the procedure has ever complained. Then again, they're too dead to speak up."

His opponent leaned over and pressed the device to the middle of Willard's forehead.

"Stop!"

Straightening, the man looked at him. "Yes?"

"I don't suppose anything I say will persuade you not to do this?"

"I'm afraid not."

"Money? Power? A job in my organization?"

"Please, Mr. Bachmann, my motives are of a higher calling."

"Ah, yes, a true believer."

"I am merely a reflection of your beliefs."

Willard gave a sigh of resignation. "I wanted to sweep away the past and bring everyone together: the vision of a harmonious future."

"That's your future, sir. That's your vision. It's harmonious in that people accept you on top, with everything and everybody else at the bottom, having just enough to get by."

"Harmony brings something for everyone. There will be inequities in life. However, the fighting that results from people not accepting that truth is the problem. Do you want war? Do you want continued conflicts between various groups vying for authority? Stopping me won't stop the system. Society is hierarchical. You can't escape it." Willard gave his foe a pleading look.

"Let us begin," the man said.

Willard sat up straight and shut his eyes in resignation. "Okay."

The man again leaned in and put one end of the tube against Willard's forehead. He pushed a button and the device hummed. A readout on one side counted out a percentage, starting at zero. The man looked around the room and, from time to time, glanced at the meter. When the number hit ninety-five, he stared at the results, keeping his thumb poised over a switch. The meter hit one hundred percent.

"Goodbye, Mr. Bachmann." The stranger pressed the button and kept the device held against Willard's forehead. There was a crunch followed by a slurping sound. Willard spasmed, all his limbs shaking at once. The man watched a long glass container within the device fill up with a viscous fluid. The counter showed a percentage once again, and when it hit one hundred, the man removed the device, exposing a hole the width of an index finger in Willard's forehead. The spasms stopped and Willard went limp, his head slumping forward onto his chest.

The man recoupled the device to his belt and removed the restraints from Willard's wrists. He picked him up and crossed the living area, stepping sideways through the door, with the body lengthwise, onto the terrace. The man followed the balustrade to the far side overlooking the plains. He looked over the rail. The building was right on the edge of the metrofloat — the perfect spot.

He lifted Willard up over the railing and let go before leaning over to watch as the body fell past fifty stories and disappeared into the blackness. With the city floating at an altitude of one kilometer, it would take Willard's body approximately fifteen seconds to hit the ground.

***

Alan and Terry were skinny enough to slip through the security perimeter into the antigravity zone. Already, they heard the pounding of the AG machines. Workers in the area often wore ear protection, as the constant noise could damage their hearing, but when one is young and foolish, protection is for wimps. They climbed down to the lowest scaffolding and looked out over the panorama below. The ground was a good kilometer down, speckled with the twinkling lights of the settlement. Each light was a potential target for a jump-and-grab, so tonight looked to be an excellent opportunity.

Rumors had been circulating around the high school for over a year about thrill seekers doing the unthinkable: bungee jumping from the metrofloat. Alan and Terry had pooled their money and bought the latest in equipment, including a controllable elasticized cable, a double-safety ankle harness, and a precision-positioning system with automatic height detection. The flexible anchor allowed them to set up the bungee in any location in record time, so they could get in, jump, and get out before the authorities knew they were violating restricted areas.

In the last few months, they had brought along groupies of the informal thrill-seekers club, and because of those witnesses, the two of them had become underground heroes. Who in their right mind would do such a thing? Tangible proof was good for their reputation, so they brought things up from their jumps. Over open land, they returned with a rock or a plant, but the real fun was over settled areas. So far, they had taken pieces of clothing drying on lines and things left out on outdoor tables, like toys and tools. Tonight, they wanted to go an extra step and steal a village marker. The other items could come from anywhere, but a sign showing the name of the community would prove they had jumped over a settlement. By using the max extension on the cable, they hoped to remain down long enough to use their tools to unfasten a sign from its support.

Alan would make the first attempt. He had decked himself with various tools attached to his belt and a helmet with a lamp. He had double-checked his ankle connectors and made sure the safety harness was in place. Terry gave him the once-over, enumerating each item out loud so they both knew they had checked everything. Alan climbed over the railing and held on as Terry fed out the cable so it was free and clear of the scaffolding.

Quivering with excitement, Alan looked over at his friend. Terry grinned and gave him a thumbs-up. Alan turned back to the open space, took a deep breath, and spread his arms out. He bent his knees and pushed off into a swan dive.

Alan had ten seconds of free fall before the cable slowed his descent — ten seconds of weightlessness as the wind whistled by his head. It was peaceful. And surreal. It wasn't every day somebody jumped from a height of a thousand meters.

Looking toward the ground when he jumped, Alan twisted as he now fell, upside down, and brought his head up to look off into the distance. The light from his helmet flashed on something. He swept his head back and forth until the object was visible again. There was a human body three meters from him, free-falling at the same rate. It tumbled in the air. Judging by the looseness of the limbs, Alan guessed the person was unconscious. Or dead. Wouldn't somebody falling to their death be thrashing about?

He looked toward the ground. The lights were coming up, and he felt the cable tense to reduce the speed of his descent.

Alan looked back at the body, which continued to fall at a steady rate and was moving away. He bent his head up so he could follow its path. There was a crash followed by a thump. *Holy crap!* This was unexpected. They had better get the hell out of there.

Alan slowed to a stop, hanging upside down two meters from the ground. He fumbled with the controller, pressing the button to ascend, and the mechanism set into motion, pulling him up. He looked back down and saw, in the semi-darkness, a hole in the roof of a nearby building. What the hell was going on?

Chapter 1

It was the oddest of sensations, although Matthew Heart didn't sort that out until later. He realized he was thinking, but he didn't know where he was and couldn't feel anything — not even his body. He felt as though he were disconnected from the outside world, floating in nothingness.

This curious state of mind lasted for a few seconds before he was plugged back into his body and a wave of nausea washed over his consciousness. The urge to retch came over him, and he tasted bile at the back of his throat. Every pain receptor in his body had been turned on, and his brain was in sensory overload. Good Lord, can a human being endure this level of agony?

Heart opened his eyes, squinting as the morning sun blazed. Thankfully, he was in the shadows. A hot, dry air enveloped him, and his entire body was sweaty. His head throbbed. Struggling into a seated position, he propped himself against something solid and hard. His gaze fell upon a whiskey bottle. It was empty. *So, a human being can consume that much alcohol and live. This is the worst of all hangovers — although, isn't the current hangover always the worst?*

Heart looked around his unfamiliar surroundings. He was leaning against a cement-block wall, and an object to his right seemed to be a trash can. When he swiveled his head, he saw other trash cans in a line. He was in an alley, but which alley?

Heart made a stumbling attempt to stand, and a renewed wave of nausea swept over him. He sat back down and let his head sink forward. *Think. Think carefully.* He'd been out at a bar the night before, having a good time, nursing a glass of artihol, when somebody had offered real alcohol. A bottle was produced, many drinks were downed for God knows what reason, and the rest was a blank.

He blinked and noticed his fly was open, his penis hanging out. He poked the end of it and tugged. He was wearing a condom. *What happened last night?*

Heart pulled the rubber off and held it up. "Oh, God."

Tossing it aside, he massaged his temples. After a moment, he used his hands to support himself in an attempt to stand and regretted it instantly. He held his head for another moment and then zipped himself up. He faltered to the street. A few pedestrians ambled by. He stood at the mouth of the alley, looking in both directions at the dusty road lined by block buildings. He wasn't far from his motel. Why wasn't he in his room? Why was he here? *Shit.* Too much, too quickly, too stupid.

Gathering his bearings, Heart shuffled a few paces down the street and plopped himself on a streetside stool at Wang's Food Bar. He plunked his elbows on the open-air counter, holding his head in both hands.

A wizened man with four tubular, mechanical limbs stood on the other side of the counter, clicking his tongue. "You're an idiot."

Heart peeked between his fingers. "Not so loud."

Wang shifted position and his robotic prosths whirred. "I saw you earlier in the alley when I took out the trash. I thought it was best to let you sleep it off."

Heart smacked his lips. "Help a poor man who's down."

Wang set a full glass of water on the counter. "Drink this. I'll fix you up with something to get you back on your feet." He scrutinized his customer. "You know, if you stuck with artihol, you wouldn't end up in this condition."

Heart continued nursing his head and said nothing.

"Alcohol can be fun, but it's a poison and you always pay the price." Wang clicked his tongue again. "Stay with something pure and proven."

"Help me or go away." Heart guzzled the entire glass of water, wiping his mouth on his sleeve as Wang disappeared to the back. He stared at the thermometer display showing forty degrees Celsius and adjusted the lapel control of his cooljack. He shut his eyes. People were doing their morning shopping. Children were playing in the street. Overhead, an antigravity vehicle, a flivver, glided past with its identifying hum. Heart didn't look; he listened, concentrating on the sounds of the morning.

Wang's metallic feet clicked, returning from the back room. There was a whirring sound followed by that of a glass being set down on the counter. "Here, this will make the bad go away."

Heart opened his eyes and focused on the glass. Picking it up, he gulped down the concoction. He winced. "What the hell was in that?"

"The original recipe calls for hot sauce, and I thought it should be twice as effective at double the amount. Now, imagine triple."

"You're a sadistic bastard." Heart gasped for breath. "Now I know why this works. The new pain distracts from the old pain. My head hurts, and your cure is to stomp on my foot." A flush shot up his neck and his nausea dissipated. "Whoa!" He stared at the glass in his hand, surprised. "What else is in this?"

"A little of this. A little of that. My secret recipe of vitamin supplements and chemical potions."

Heart thumped the counter with the empty glass. "Wang, you're a genius."

"From now on, stick to artihol. No alcohol; only synthetics."

Heart held up one hand and crossed his heart with the other. "On my mother's grave."

Wang sneered. "Yeah, right."

"How about breakfast, now that I feel human again?"

Wang walked off and stationed himself at the grill.

As Heart sat, waiting, he heard a strange noise. He spun around on his stool and then remembered his communicator and touched the side of his ear-tab. A screen came out of the device and curved around his right eye. The integrated display lit up, showing an incoming call. "Answer."

The display flickered before showing the image of Decker, the precinct dispatcher. "Detective Heart, did you find your way home last night?"

Heart debated whether he should answer. His position would have been logged from his ID chip, and anybody could guess why he had spent the past six hours in an alley. It wasn't the first time. The problem with having a reputation. "What do you want?"

"I'm just the messenger." Decker held up both hands in a "who, me?" gesture and grinned. "Chief Hooper would like to see your smiling countenance in the office as soon as possible."

Heart looked at the time. "Give me forty-five."

"Okey-dokey." Decker hung up and Heart touched the ear-tab. The display disappeared.

Wang set a partially filled plate on the counter that included a slice of flatbread.

Heart poked the stringy mixture with a fork. "What's this?"

"Today's special: mealworm stew." Wang turned away and picked up a frying pan.

"Oh, great! My appetite has come back." Heart popped several larvae in his mouth and smacked his lips. "Mmm, delicious."

Wang tilted the sizzling pan and used a spatula to slide the contents onto Heart's plate.

"No crickets?"

"Nope. Locust. Fresh this morning."

Heart pinched an insect between his thumb and index finger, biting off its head and half the body. As he crunched on it, he took another forkful of stew. "You know how to make a plate, Wang. The best insects in town."

"I do what I can." Wang walked back to the grill and set down the pan.

Heart was engrossed in his meal when he heard noise from up the street. He turned to see a scuffle that had broken out between a woman and a teenage boy. The boy was standing on running blades and tugging at the woman's shopping bag. The woman held tight and yelled. The boy yanked with one hand and pushed the woman with the other. She lost her balance and fell backward, letting go of the bag. The boy half ran, half bounced down the street as the woman shrieked. Several people gave chase.

Heart tore off a bite of flatbread and spun on his stool,

sticking out a leg as the boy reached the counter. The boy tripped and fell headlong onto the street, dropping the bag. One pursuer retrieved it as others stood over the boy, scolding him. "Shame on you, thief! Stealing from a woman!" The group trudged back to the victim.

Job done, Heart turned back to his breakfast and continued to eat. He watched out of the corner of his eye as the boy got up, brushed himself off, and stomped off in a huff.

Wang looked up from the grill. "Yerba mate?"

"Sure," Heart said.

Wang filled a metal gourd with tea leaves, pouring in warm water from a kettle. As he approached Heart, he grabbed a bombilla from a shelf and stuck it in the drink. "Let it steep," he said, setting the gourd on the counter before returning to the grill.

Heart swirled the bombilla around with one hand as he took a forkful of stew with the other. As he picked up the drink and sipped, a hand fell on his shoulder and twirled his stool around. Heart moved the sloshing beverage away from himself and looked up to find a large man standing over him, scowling.

"Are you the prick who tripped my brother?"

Heart glanced behind the man and saw the grinning teenage boy. The man poked Heart's shoulder with a robotic index finger. "You should mind your own business. People like you find themselves in a lot of trouble."

Heart held the man's gaze. Without looking away, he set the gourd down and dabbed a finger on the corner of his mouth.

"Are you deaf?" The man put his other hand, a human hand, against a supporting beam and leaned toward Heart. "I think you owe my brother an apology. In fact, I think you owe my brother something more." The man poked Heart's shoulder with a mechanical finger again and held his palm up, wiggling his fingers in the universal gesture of a request for money.

Heart heard a dull thump and turned his head to look at the supporting beam. There, between the third and fourth fingers of the man's hand, was a butcher's knife. The handle quivered.

"Bugger off," Wang said.

The man glared at Wang and then looked down at Heart, who pulled back his jacket to reveal a concealed shoulder holster. Heart raised his brows as the man looked at the gun and scowled. Grabbing the teenage boy by the arm, the man hauled his brother away.

"What?" the teenager whined at his brother. "Aren't you going to hit him or something?"

"Shut up," the man said. They disappeared down the street.

Heart turned back to the counter. "Thanks."

Wang pulled his knife out of the beam. "You love getting yourself into trouble."

"What? Me?" Heart gave a mock look of innocence. "I'm for truth, justice, and ladies with shopping bags."

Wang pointed at him with the knife. "From now on, no alcohol. You hear?"

"Yes, sir." Heart pushed his plate back and picked at his front teeth with his pinkie finger. He looked at the locust leg on the tip and then flicked it away with his thumb. "Time to go to work."

Wang held up a small device. "Time to pay, you mean."

Heart pressed his thumb on the POS.

"And?" Wang said, sneering.

"And what?"

"I saved you from getting your face slapped. That isn't worth something? Never mind sparing you from twenty-four hours of hangover hell."

Heart fiddled with the touchscreen. "Twenty percent."

Wang clicked his tongue in disgust. "I would have said twenty-five at least. Now, get lost." Wang trudged off to the other end of the counter.

The detective headed off to work.

***

FS45, Farm Settlement Forty-Five, had a population of fifteen thousand and a police force of twenty-seven — a typical ratio of citizens to officers. However, this was anything but a typical society. Most of the people, the grounders, were transient workers looking to scrape together a quick credit and spend those credits on entertainment: artihol, gambling, and an old type of singing called karaoke. This was a busy community, but busy didn't always translate into good.

Matthew Heart, detective first class, arrived at Headquarters, an undistinguished, two-story building made from cement block, like most other settlement buildings. Looking at his reflection in the glass window of the main door, he ran a hand through his hair. He unbuttoned his cooljack, tugged at the lapels, and polished the toe of each boot on the back of a pant leg. Holding one hand over his mouth and nose, he exhaled and winced. This wasn't his best, but it would have to do. He put a thumb on a scan panel and, hearing a click, pulled open the door and entered the lobby.

"Detective Heart, how good to see you." Decker grinned at him from behind a secure window.

Heart nodded. He didn't mind the man but sometimes felt violated; his privacy wasn't all that private. The precinct monitored all officers, their positions logged to better provide backup in case of emergency. He didn't like that everybody knew when he was jacking off in the can, but that was better than finding himself alone with an angry crowd of bad guys.

"Hooper's expecting you. Go right in."

"Okay."

Heart pressed his thumb to another scanner to get into the main part of the building, climbed the stairs to the second floor, and walked down a hall toward the inspector's office. He knocked on the door and waited. A muffled voice responded, so he entered and found Hooper standing at the window with a woman. They turned.

"Detective Heart, come in. I would like you to meet Sergeant Elizabeth Stanton."

As Heart looked at the woman, the hairs on the back of his neck stood up. Stanton, hair cropped short, was an imposing figure looming over Hooper. She was immaculate in a white Metrofloat New York police uniform, a crisp jacket and pants. Her face was expressionless, with no hint of friendliness. "Ms. Stanton," Heart said. The word was out of his mouth so quickly he at first didn't realize his blunder. The woman looked at him with what he interpreted as the urge to kill. "I mean, Sergeant Stanton." Heart stuck out his hand, but she ignored it and looked away.

"Heart is our number one investigator," Hooper said.

Stanton returned her gaze, inspecting Heart from head to toe. "Really?" She pointed to the front of his shirt. "I'm glad to see you dressed up."

Heart peered down. There was a stain but he also looked rumpled, having slept all night in his clothes. In fact, he appeared grubby. "I..." He froze, trying to think of an explanation. "Uh, sorry." Taking a step back from Stanton, his foot caught a bump in the concrete floor. He lost his balance and fell backward.

Hooper looked alarmed. "Heart, are you all right? Get up, man." He rolled his eyes and pointed to Stanton. "Sergeant Stanton's arrived from Metrofloat New York. She's here to investigate the disappearance of Willard Bachmann."

Heart got up and tugged on his jacket, casting a quizzical look at the floor. "That name's familiar."

"Bachmann was the most powerful man on the metrofloat," Stanton said. "He was poised to become the next leader of the OligCouncil."

"We here in the settlements do get the news."

Stanton ignored him. "Bachmann failed to show up for a meeting this morning. When his personal aide went to find him, he found the apartment empty, but the door to the terrace was open."

"Did he jump?" Heart asked.

"That would seem unlikely."

"Found a body?"

"We may have."

"Here? In FS45?"

Hooper reached over his desk and picked up a hand-tab. "Dispatch received a call this morning from a Mr. and Mrs. Mortimer, who reported discovering a body, or what they think is a body. They're not sure."

Heart looked at Stanton. "You think that's Bachmann?"

"We know Bachmann is no longer in New York. Since we did a float-by last night, we're expanding our search to cover this area."

Heart reached to take the tab from Hooper but couldn't get it out from his grip. He pulled. It wouldn't budge, and Heart raised his brows at the chief.

Hooper growled at his outstretched arm. "Damn." Reaching up with his free hand, he banged on his arm and then grabbed hold of his thumb and pulled up. "Take the tab, Heart."

Heart yanked on the tab. "Got it."

"Crap technology." Hooper struggled with his arm, trying to push it down. Finally, he reached into his armpit and fiddled with something. The arm fell to his side.

Stanton looked on with a slight smile. "Is that a Mark III?"

Hooper grumbled. "Yes."

"The Mark IV has redundant systems."

"Like I could afford that on my salary." Hooper fiddled with a desk-tab. "I'm going to the shop to get this fixed." He pointed out the window. "Heart, I want you to take Sergeant Stanton over to check out this body."

"Yes, sir."

Hooper was already on a call. "Freddy, I'm coming over right now. This piece of crap has given out on me again."

Heart gestured to the door. "Shall we?"

"He should get the Mark IV," Stanton said as the two exited the office.

"Unfortunately, Sergeant, such items are pricey in the settlements. The people out here don't make all that much, so they would have a tough time affording it even in the city."

"Oh?"

"Farmers are a poor lot. This is manual labor at its best. But on top of that, farmers have the highest rate of necrofasc on the planet. At least ninety-five percent of all the people in this community have a prosth. About a third have lost more than one limb, and one in ten have lost all four. And I haven't even mentioned those with artificial organs. Some people are more machine than human."

Stanton said nothing as they left the precinct building. Heart gestured to the passenger door of a police flivver and slid into the driver's seat. The entire machine came alive, activated by his embedded ID. "We have a ride to the outskirts of town, Sergeant." He linked the car's console to the precinct report and selected the destination. A warning buzzer sounded, and the auto-belts slid into place. Another buzzer sounded as the onboard navigator took control. The car rose straight up, turned, and headed southeast at a height of thirty meters. Heart could see the edge of town, the plains stretching beyond. Far off in the distance was Metrofloat New York, drifting in the winds.

"You're whole," Stanton said.

"Just lucky."

"You have no replacements?"

"That's right."

"I'm impressed. You're a rarity." Stanton stared out the window. "It's a sign of status to be whole in the city — nothing artificial, everything real. People pay a premium to get replacement parts."

"So I've heard. There's a black market in the settlements. People here are poor, and they're willing to give up a limb or an organ for a price. I'm not sure it's a good trade-off, considering the price of a good prosth. Hooper doesn't have the state of the art, as you pointed out, and he couldn't afford it. Some have mechanical attachments, not even artificial limbs."

"How did you escape the necrofasc?"

"Good genes?" He tapped a finger on the console. "While I was in the military, I gave blood samples as part of a study to better understand why one in a hundred thousand showed resistance to the mutated bacteria. I've heard there are new antibiotics, but the best treatment — or should I say the cheapest? — is to remove the infected flesh. So much for modern life. If it weren't for biotechnology, many people would live out their lives minus body parts."

"Yes, you give up a little of your humanity."

After a moment of silence, Heart glanced at Stanton. She appeared lost in thought. "How did you get assigned to this case?"

"Somebody recommended me. It wasn't my idea."

"How could you pass up an opportunity to visit our wonderful settlement?"

"I do as I'm told."

"We all have a master."

The car began its descent toward a group of low-rise buildings on the edge of town. Behind the main building, six utility warehouses stretched into the distance. Beyond them were squares of farmed land.

"What is this place?" Stanton asked.

"EntomoCorp. It's their largest cricket farm," Heart said, pointing to a sign over the main entrance.

"Oh?"

"You've never seen one?"

"I'm a city dweller. I admit I've never traveled."

"Well, this is your chance to see where your food comes from."

They entered the main building and found the office.

"Are you Antonio?"

A man looked up from his desk. "Yeah?"

"Detective Heart from the precinct. You called in a body?"

Antonio stood and shook Heart's hand. "Thanks for coming."

Heart gestured to Stanton. "This is Sergeant Stanton of MetPol."

Antonio nodded in greeting. "I've seen nothing like this. The morning shift reported it." He pulled open a side door. "Let me take you out back."

They crossed a concrete-tiled rectangular yard and headed to the farthest warehouse, marked Barn No.1. Antonio held the door and ushered them in. Rows of elongated tubs extended the length of the building, attended by various workers scattered throughout the complex.

"Follow me to the back," Antonio said as he led them down the central aisle.

Stanton cocked her head, surprised. "The chirping."

Heart chuckled. "Yes. You've never visited a farm."

Without breaking stride, Antonio waved his hand around the complex. "We estimate we have a quarter of a billion insects in this barn. Crews work constantly: feeding, harvesting, and cleaning, through a staggered six-week cycle. Most of this product is processed and packaged for the city."

Heart and Stanton followed, listening.

Antonio pointed to the nearest row of bins. "The insects live in cricket condos: corrugated plastic constructions. Free-range living with all the cornmeal they can eat. Then it's off for freeze-dry euthanasia, where they're packaged whole or ground into flour. I'm sure you've eaten our product."

"Humph," Stanton said.

Antonio continued to discuss aspects of the operations. It took five minutes to walk the length of the building. At the end, they came to a sliding door as high as the ceiling, where, off to one side, an elderly couple sat on a bench next to a table. The woman, whose long white hair fell halfway down her back, had two mechanical arms. The stooped, balding man had all four limbs replaced with mechanical prosthetics. They both struggled to stand and gave an expectant smile.

"Mr. and Mrs. Mortimer," Antonio said, "this is Detective Heart and Sergeant Stanton." He turned to Heart. "The Mortimers work in our processing section. They discovered the body."

"It happened last night," Mr. Mortimer said.

"Yes, it did. I heard it, too," Mrs. Mortimer said.

"Heard what?" Heart asked.

Mr. Mortimer gestured to the door. "We might as well

show you."

"Yes," Mrs. Mortimer said. "Show them."

Antonio slid the door open and they all entered a shop populated by machines and workbenches. At the far end stood a garage door with a loading dock.

"Look," Mr. Mortimer said.

Mrs. Mortimer pointed. "Yes, look."

There, in the middle of the floor, was a splatter of flesh. It took a moment, but Heart guessed it was a human body. He looked up at a ragged hole in the roof.

Stanton was about to take a step when she saw a dark red spot on the floor. She shifted her foot and continued around the body.

"What time did you hear this?" Stanton asked.

"During the middle of the night," Mr. Mortimer said.

"Yes," Mrs. Mortimer said. "During the night."

"But we didn't think of getting up to investigate." Mr. Mortimer pointed to the outside. "We live next door and we hear stuff out here, what with the late-night shifts, so we didn't think anything of it."

Mrs. Mortimer opened her mouth to speak, but instead, her husband beamed at her and patted her shoulder.

As Heart gingerly stepped around the area, Stanton held out a device and scanned the main part of the mass. "Total body disruption. I can't get a reading on the ID. The impact must have knocked out the chip. I can't even register it. I'm wondering if we're missing the left arm."

Heart looked up at the hole in the ceiling. "Was it torn off when the body crashed through the roof?"

Stanton followed his gaze. "Could be. Let's go have a look." She turned to the Mortimers. "Do you have a ladder?"

"Yes," Mr. Mortimer said. He picked his way to the open garage door and moved outside. Heart and Stanton followed, watching as Mr. Mortimer set up a ladder against the side of the building.

Heart put one hand on the ladder. "After you, Sergeant."

Stanton looked at Heart and, without a hint of emotion,

climbed up. Heart followed and found himself on a flat roof punctuated by vertical air vents. They each examined the surrounding area, skirting the hole.

Heart peered around one of the vertical tubes and called to Stanton. "I found part of an arm."

As Stanton turned and headed toward him, there was an audible crack and Heart felt one foot go through the roofing. Losing his balance, he threw out his arms, trying to grab something solid. There was a rumble as part of the roof gave way and a large hole opened. Heart panicked as he tipped over and tumbled through.

Yet, midair, he stopped falling and found himself dangling by one arm. He was being pulled back up and turned his head to look. Stanton held his right wrist and lifted him back onto the roof. She gripped an air vent to anchor herself, using the other arm to raise him to safety.

"Thanks," Heart said, puzzled at her uncommon strength.

Stanton headed back down the ladder. "Let's go. I believe that was the missing left arm."

Back in the shop, Stanton crouched over the limb and studied the readout from a device. "This is Willard Bachmann, no doubt about it. The chip matches." She stood. "I'll call in a forensics team. We'll want to cordon off the area and do a thorough search for remaining body parts."

"I'll phone Hooper for clearance," Heart said.

Stanton looked at him. "Technically, Hooper reports to Metrofloat New York. But, yes, as a courtesy."

When Stanton turned away, he shook his head in disapproval. *Who does she think she is?* Then again, everyone reported to the city.

An hour later, Hooper and Heart stood across from the warehouse, hands shielding their eyes from the sunlight. There were eight police flivvers, and a larger vehicle marked Forensics, parked by the loading dock. A dozen people with scanners wandered around the area. Off to one side, a police officer interviewed the Mortimers.

"When do you think they'll finish?" Heart asked.

Hooper stood with his arms crossed, one hand on his chin. "I'll guess a couple of hours. They've done a sweep, but they'll do a couple more to be sure they haven't missed anything. This Bachmann guy was important, so I'm certain Headquarters has told them to be extra thorough. If it's suicide, everything can be wrapped up quickly. But if it's murder, as the sergeant has suggested, this could go on for a while. Whatever the case, I'd say the answer is in Bachmann's apartment."

Sergeant Stanton came from behind the house and strode over to Hooper and Heart. "It's definitely murder."

"How can you tell?" Heart asked.

"There's no brain."

"Pardon?" Heart and Hooper looked at each other in disbelief.

"Forensics found the head — well, what's left of it. And after examining the remains, they concluded the brain had been removed from the skull. Somebody dumped the body from Bachmann's terrace. The logs of his ID show him to be in his apartment last night."

"Why would they take the brain?"

"Because there is now no way of reconstructing memory to find out who the killer was. But more importantly, removing the brain means the killer stole Bachmann's memories. His knowledge is gone. We can't access his secrets."

Heart scratched his forehead. "What's this got to do with anything?"

"I told you Bachmann was to become the next head of the OligCouncil. Somebody didn't want that to happen."

"The powerful are duking it out. That's above my pay grade."

"Mine, too," Stanton said. "I stay away from politics."

Hooper gestured. "So, Sergeant Stanton, I take it this is now in your capable hands. We here in FS45 can get back to our own concerns."

"Once the forensics team finishes up, I see no reason for us to come back. But there is one more request from upstairs."

"Oh?" Hooper raised an eyebrow.

"Somebody asked to see Detective Heart."

Hooper looked at Heart. "Who? Why?"

"I can't say why," Stanton said, "but I can tell you who." She paused, the two men expectant. "Voynich."

Heart rolled his eyes. "Michael Voynich?"

"Who's that?" Hooper asked.

"When I did my stint in the military, Voynich was my commander. I thought he had it in for me. After I took a discharge, I lost track of him but then heard he'd been promoted."

"Michael Voynich is now chief security officer of Metrofloat New York," Stanton said.

"Impressive," Hooper said. "I wonder what he wants with you, Detective."

Heart shook his head. "This can't be good."

Stanton looked at Heart's clothes. "Voynich wants me to bring you back for an audience. Do you have anything more formal to wear?"

"How long do I have, Sergeant Stanton?"

She looked in the direction of the forensics team. "I'd say another three hours."

"Fine. I'll go home and change. How about you pick me up at the precinct, let's say at sixteen hundred?"

"Sixteen hundred." Stanton turned and walked away.

Chapter 2

Heart plodded home from the precinct, his shades on max in the blazing sun. It was hot. It was dry. Each step kicked up dust.

"Hello, Matthew."

He turned to see a woman smoking in a doorway. Her arti-arm took the cigarette from her mouth, and she blew a smoke ring.

"Hi, Jessica," he said, stopping. "Still smoking."

"Hey, we all have bad habits. Fortunately, my new arti-lungs are self-cleaning, so I no longer have to worry about a cough."

He nodded.

"Speaking of bad habits, what happened to you last night?" Jessica eyed him.

"What do you mean?"

"You left the party early. I thought we were going to do business."

"Sorry, I was a little drunk. I don't know who switched us from artihol to alcohol, but that was a mistake. Ugh!"

She chuckled. "A little drunk? You have a gift of understatement. I figure you've got to be hungover bad."

"Wang gave me one of his miracle cures."

"Lucky you." She took a puff. "My offer still stands."

"Offer?"

"I'll do you for free. You're whole, and the feel of real flesh is a treat."

He smiled and kissed her cheek. "You're not going to get rich, Jessica, giving it away for free."

"I'm on the ground. I'll never be rich. I'm just hoping for comfortable."

"That's something we should all strive for." He stepped back. "Time to go to work. Take care of yourself, Jessica."

"Thanks. You, too."

His home was a one-bedroom at the Low Cost Lodge. The word *lodge* sounded exotic, but like most of the buildings in the settlement, it was plain and functional: a two-story, cement-block structure. The apartment had a kitchenette and provided the basics, nothing luxurious. But, here in FS45, that was good.

Heart climbed the stairs and went down the dimly lit hall. His footsteps clicked on the concrete floor as he approached a girl in her early teens sitting on the floor with a backpack. "Sally, what are you doing out here?"

"Mom's at work, and I can't get in. I think the door's broken." She brushed her blonde hair aside with one hand.

"Show me."

Sally stood on one real leg, balancing herself with a non-mechanical prosthetic. She hobbled to the door and put her thumb on the scanner. The light stayed red, and there was a beep.

Heart bent over and looked at the touch pad. Licking the end of his finger, he cleaned the surface and then pulled out a shirttail and wiped it down. "Try it now."

She tried her thumb again. The light on the door turned green, and there was the audible click of the door unlocking. "Hey, Matty, thanks! I'll have to try that the next time this happens."

"No problem," he said. "Say, why are you home in the middle of the day? What happened to school?"

"The teacher was called away to the farm, and we got out early. Do you want to have lunch with me?"

"Soup?"

"What else can I cook?"

"You make a good sandwich."

"Anybody can do that."

Heart followed her into the apartment. "What's your class working on now?"

"History." She put her pack on the table.

"What history?"

"The teacher's telling us about the Pandemic."

"What did he say?"

"He told us there were once fifteen billion people on Earth, but in a year, twelve billion died." Sally opened a cupboard and pointed to a shelf.

"Yes. My grandparents lived through it." He took down two bowls and sat at the table. "They were lucky."

"What happened?" Sally busied herself, moving between the counter and the microwave.

"Cities were abandoned. Entire countries disappeared. So many people died, the living couldn't keep up, and it turned into a fight for survival. Today, you can visit areas that are giant morgues. Dead people were left in the open because there was nobody left to bury the bodies."

"Have you been there?"

"Yeah, I've visited several places. 'Float New York is named after an abandoned city now partially flooded by the ocean. That city is deserted — a tomb for forty million people."

"Wasn't there any medicine?"

"Bacteria and viruses mutate — they change. Medicine stops working, and science must find new medicines. That's why people took to the skies."

"The floaters?"

"Yes. Antigravity — AG — was invented before the Pandemic. It became the new way not just to travel, but to live. Airplanes disappeared. They were no longer needed."

"What's an airplane?"

"It was a machine for flying."

"Like a bird?"

"Sort of. We used to have wings to fly. Now we have AG to float."

Sally set two steaming bowls on the table.

Heart grinned. "I'm hungry."

"Me too," Sally said, setting a plastic bag in the middle of the table. "Do you want crickets?"

"Sure." Heart took a few insects from the bag as he spooned the soup.

"With the climate getting hotter," he said, "floating platforms were a way of escaping the heat. Rich people created homes, and then communities, so they could enjoy a moderate temperature at a higher altitude. Plus, it was a way to have better security from crime."

"History's kind of boring."

He chuckled. "I had to learn all this stuff in school like you're doing."

She watched him as she chewed a cricket.

"The platforms turned into the best way to escape the Pandemic and then later the necrofasc. Did you know there are other platforms besides New York and Los Angeles? Chongqing, Shanghai, Delhi, Tokyo, London, Paris, Rome. People everywhere left the ground. Well, those who could afford it."

"Why are you whole?"

"Nobody knows yet. For some reason, my body has an immunity to the bacteria. But most people eventually get infected. Well, I should say grounders do. Floaters don't get necrofasc. The bacteria exists on the ground, and if you never visit the ground you never get it. There are treatments and ways to avoid it, but those cost money and grounders can't afford it. Their solution is amputation. Not much of a choice, but it's better than dying."

"I've lost a leg. Will I lose something else?"

"I'd like to tell you a feel-good story, but nobody knows for sure. Usually, necrofasc attacks the body only once. So, if you've been infected and had something removed, there's a good chance it won't happen again." He pointed his spoon for emphasis. "However, I've known people who got infected several times. It's amazing how good artificial body parts are now: legs, arms, eyes, even internal organs. But the problem for all grounders is cost. You can have it if you can afford it, and if you can't afford it you go without — or you get something less expensive."

"My arti-leg isn't good."

"Your mother wants to wait for you to grow more. A good leg isn't cheap, and she can't afford to buy something new each year. You're sprouting."

"I think I look ugly," Sally said.

"What?" Heart looked at her, startled. "How can you say that? You're a pretty girl."

"It's not a human leg."

"And who said human is better? Wang can easily beat me at arm wrestling, and he can outrun me." He snorted. "And who said human even looks better? I can't imagine Wang with human limbs. I told him not to waste his credits getting arti-flesh. He looks fine just the way he is."

"But Mom got arti-flesh," Sally said.

"I know. She felt better having to deal with the wholes who come from the city. That's fine. It's like getting dressed up. But it doesn't matter to me. I accept her the way she is." He patted Sally's arm. "And I accept you. You're perfect just the way you are." Heart paused and bit down on another insect. "Mmm, love that. Did you know people didn't always eat insects?"

Sally glanced around. "But what else is there?"

"People used to eat animals."

"Eew! That's disgusting!"

Heart laughed. "The Pandemic affected anything warm-blooded. That meant humans and animals. Along with all the people who died, just about every animal disappeared. In a short time, the remaining people had to find other sources of food. Yeah there were fish, but that wasn't enough. Some people had been eating insects off and on for thousands of years, but the Pandemic turned insects into the main source of food for everyone. When you have no choice, you can change."

"My teacher never mentioned that."

"I'm an endless source of sundry facts. Mention it in class and you'll get yourself an A." Heart looked at Sally's bowl. "Are you finished?"

"Yes."

He picked up the two bowls and took them to the sink. "You made lunch, so I'll clean up. Deal?"

"Deal."

Heart checked the time. "But after that, I have to go back to work. Are you going to be all right by yourself?"

"I'm a big girl."

"That you are."

"Mom will check in with me. She said she'd be home when she takes a supper break."

"Okay. I'll catch you later. Say hello to your mom for me."

"Thanks, Matty."

"Any time. Thank you for lunch." Heart walked a few doors down, entered his suite, and set about getting himself cleaned up with a shower and a shave. He knew he had a suit somewhere in the back of his closet.

Fifteen minutes later, Heart was putting the finishing touches on his best outfit. After giving himself a quick, final check in the mirror, he headed back to the precinct.

***

Stanton looked him up and down upon arrival. "Better."

"Thank you. I'll try to make a good impression by not tripping."

"I'll look forward to seeing that." She motioned toward the flivver.

"How far do we have to go?"

"The metrofloat is now a hundred and twenty kilometers to the southeast."

As the car rose, Heart could make out their destination in the distance.

"I'm surprised you managed to pull me up to safety earlier. City folk aren't usually enhanced," he said.

She flinched but continued to look straight ahead. "I'm not enhanced."

"Pardon?"

Stanton curled her lip. "I'm a synth."

"What?"

She turned to him, her cheeks flushed. "You heard me. I'm an artif, a cyborg."

"Sorry. I've heard of artifs, but I've never met one."

Stanton turned back to the controls. "Great. You're no

longer a virgin."

"Listen, I didn't mean anything by that," he said, glancing out the window. "If you don't mind me asking, what happened?"

Stanton fiddled with a control.

"If you don't want to talk about it..."

"No, I'll tell you. You'll find out eventually." She sighed. "Like you, I served my time in the military. There was an accident." She wouldn't look at him. "I was part of a squad, training with live ordnance. Something blew up. When I woke, I was a brain. Nothing else of myself had survived. I have no idea why, but Special Programs decided to do something with me instead of letting me die. They gave me this synth body."

"I had no idea."

"Most people don't. That is, at least not from a distance. When you get close, some people can tell."

Intrigued by the engineering, he leaned over and looked closer.

She winced. "I discovered people feel uncomfortable around me. I'm a freak to them."

"In the settlements, I've seen it all. Heck, most people there have nothing of the quality you have. Sometimes their prosths have no skin, with all the inner mechanics exposed. You'd make them jealous."

"Don't forget, I live and work in the city. Being human, comprised of real human parts, is a prized possession. You're considered upper class if you're 'whole.' I'm no longer whole. I'm the opposite of whole."

"It's no big deal to me."

"My colleagues work with me willingly enough — they're professionals. But on a personal level, people don't associate with me."

"As I said, Sergeant Stanton, it's okay." Heart tapped an index finger on his temple. "It's what's up here that counts."

She gave a sideways glance. "Those are kind words, Detective Heart, but truth is in actions. In the city, being human counts for everything, and if you're not completely human you're considered of lesser status."

"Why don't you call me Matthew? We have a long trip ahead of us."

Stanton looked sober. "Okay." She stuck out a hand. "Elizabeth, but only for now."

Heart shook her hand, grinning. "Fair enough. I'll endeavor to take advantage of this personal moment."

She sighed. "I'm alive, and for that I'm grateful. But I'm afraid becoming a synth meant giving up my humanity to a certain extent. As I said, I'm considered a freak. People shy away from freaks, and intimacy is out of the question."

"I'm sorry."

"Don't be sorry. Life is how it is."

"In the settlements, we're more accepting. Everybody's different in one way or another."

"Sounds like heaven. But I don't think I want to aim for that level of poverty."

"Hey, none of those people asked to be poor. Sometimes things happen. And not all of us are born floaters."

Stanton remained silent. "Okay, now it's my turn to apologize."

"No prob." Heart idly scanned the fields whizzing by under the flying car.

"So, what happened to *you*?"

"What do you mean?"

"I looked you up," she said. "You did a good tour in the military and then worked in the city. How did you end up in an FS with the local police?"

"I pissed somebody off. Somebody with power."

"Voynich?"

"Nah, he wasn't around then. I stopped a corporate bigwig from mistreating a woman. He kicked my ass to the ground, and I've been in the settlement ever since. Lucky for me I found a place in law and order. It beats farming."

"There may be law, but I've heard there's lack of order. Something of an untamed wilderness."

Heart shrugged. "True, but there are a lot of good people

on the ground. Their only crime is poverty."

"You never thought to get back to the city?"

"After being declared *persona non grata*, I thought it wasn't worth the pain of bucking the system. Us little folk need to stay out of the way of the big boys."

Heart had been staring out the front window, watching the ever-growing metrofloat with a mix of trepidation and excitement. He'd been away a long time, but he remained impressed by its towering metal and glass structures, floating over the Earth as an ethereal paradise. It was magnificent, and it was what grounders aspired to.

"Squad car one-four-three-two, route to Central. Meeting with Voynich at seventeen hundred."

Stanton put a finger on a touchscreen. "Roger, Dispatch."

"That means aerial Henry Hudson to the new exit at West Fifty-Seventh and then jog over to Columbus," Heart said.

"Very good, Detective Heart. You remember your way around."

He glanced at her. "Elizabeth is over?"

"Back to work."

The flivver entered the southwest portal, docking for two minutes for decontamination. Stanton input their destination and the autopilot linked to Highway Control. The central system took over command of the vehicle and routed it to the desired address.

"Not much has changed," Stanton said. "The HQ tower still houses both police and military, but there's little need for the military. Trade is more profitable than war, and no other floats in the world have the time or resources to dabble in conflict. We're all too busy trying to survive."

The flivver stopped at the main entrance. Stanton and Heart got out, the car gliding away to autopark. Heart took a deep breath. "Cool and fresh. What a change from the ground!"

They walked through a door and into the public foyer.

Stanton continued on for a few steps before realizing she was alone and looked back. "Coming?"

"It's been a long time." He stood gazing up at the domed ceiling, thinking of the times he had crossed this lobby.

"Who knows? You may find your way back here." They entered an elevator and Stanton faced the console. "Voynich."

A melodious voice announced, "Chief Voynich, floor thirty-four. Going up."

Heart watched the display of floor numbers flicker as the car rose. "Have you ever met the chief?"

"No."

"Intimidated?"

She frowned. "No. Why?"

"I don't know. Head of operations, the big man. We, the little people."

"The police force is an organization with structure and discipline. I see no reason to be intimidated by others. We all have a role to play."

"We're all intimidated by something," Heart said.

"What?"

A bell chimed and the melodious voice said, "Floor thirty-four. Chief Voynich."

The doors opened and they got off the elevator. Stanton walked to a nearby desk and addressed the attendant. "Sergeant Stanton and Detective Heart, here to see Chief Voynich."

"One moment." The attendant closed a file on an interactive screen before standing and walking around his desk. "If you would follow me, Chief Voynich will see you now." The man pressed his thumb onto a panel beside a door. After a moment, there was a ring and the door opened. He gestured an invitation for them to enter.

Stanton and Heart marched into a spacious office, one side with floor-to-ceiling windows giving a view of the downtown core. A distinguished older gentleman with a beard got up from the desk and came around to meet them.

"Sergeant Stanton," Voynich said sticking out his hand.

Stanton shook it. "Sir."

"Detective Heart." Voynich next offered his hand to Heart.

Heart shook it. "Chief Voynich."

Voynich stared at him. "It's been a long time."

"Yes, it has."

"I was sorry to hear about the demotion."

Heart stiffened.

"Unfortunately, there was nothing I could do at the time. Powerful people have powerful friends, and what's fair isn't always what happens." Clasping his hands behind his back, Voynich sauntered over to the window. "I'd like to rectify that." He stared out at the metrofloat. "Join me."

Heart and Stanton looked at one another, confused, and then Heart went to stand beside Voynich.

Voynich glanced behind. "You too, Stanton."

He gestured to the city. "There are thirty million people out there. Thirty million individuals living their own lives. All of us are part of the city, and we get what we need from the system: food, shelter, and safety. In return, we give back with taxes, labor, and consumption. It's a symbiotic relationship. One depends on the other, and it's a delicate balance. If that balance were upset, it wouldn't be good for the system, nor for the individuals. Chaos could erupt, and with it, our way of life."

Voynich smiled knowingly. "Greed is a good thing. But let me qualify that." He turned to face Heart and Stanton. "Our desire to better ourselves, get material things, and raise our standard of living is a good thing. It motivates us to try harder. However, the desire to obtain, if left unchecked, can turn into greed. How much does any one person need to be happy? What if your desire to increase your riches becomes detrimental to others? What if others suffer so you can have more?"

He crossed his arms. "Crime is down, but a city this size has its share of murders. The death of Willard Bachmann is not another statistic. Bachmann was one of the most important people in Metrofloat New York. As the next leader of the OligCouncil, he would have become the most powerful man in the city. There is no doubt his death is a sign of something much larger. Rumors have been flying around for some time of a conspiracy to upset the status quo. The council has, at times, appeared to be a bunch of petulant school children vying to be head of the playground, but such is the nature of large egos clashing over who's right. This, however, changes the game. There could be truth to the gossip of one member wanting to wrest all power away from the council and turn it into a dictatorship." Voynich looked back out the window. "This is where you come in."

"Sir?" Heart said.

"I need somebody outside the normal structure. With any organization there's bound to be some corruption. We do our best, but such is human nature. Corruption, bribery, favors — all are in play when you get a bunch of people working together. I doubt we'll ever see the end of it. It's what people do. I want the two of you to investigate, but I want this to be hush-hush. You'll report directly to me. I'll make sure everybody in the chain of command knows this is a special assignment, and you'll get clearance for anything and everything. But in saying that, I want you to know I'm painting a target on you. Anybody who's working in the shadows, putting together a coup, will know what I'm doing by bringing you in. They won't want to show their hand, but that won't stop them from lashing out if you get too close to the truth."

Voynich pointed out the window. "There's a murderer out there. I want you to find him... or her. Remember, this person isn't just a murderer: they are a potential dictator. They're plotting something big, and I'm sure they'll stop at nothing to get their way. Too much is at stake. Everything is at stake. The life of any one man" — Voynich looked at Stanton — "or woman means nothing to them."

Finished, Voynich walked back to his desk and sat down. "Detective Heart?"

Heart stepped forward. "Yes, sir?"

"I want you to see Captain Cranston. He'll get you plugged back into the system and brief you on the case."

Heart looked at the older man. "Yes, sir."

Voynich busied himself at a display, pressing and swiping his fingers across the screen. "And Sergeant Stanton?"

"Yes, sir?" She came forward.

"All your other duties are canceled. I'm assigning you to this case. Heart is now your full-time partner."

Stanton looked at Heart and then back at Voynich. "Yes, sir." She remained expressionless, but her jaw clenched.

"I expect a report every day at seventeen hundred hours." Voynich picked up a small rectangular box. "This communicator is encrypted and linked to a similar device in my possession. These are the only two in existence with this eighty-one ninety-two-bit certificate. Call me, twenty-four seven, if anything significant crops up. I'll have this on me at all times." He held the device out to Heart.

Heart took it, turning it over in his hand. "I'm surprised you're calling on me."

"Why?"

"I had the impression you didn't like me."

Voynich pushed himself back in his seat and stroked his beard. "It was my job to push recruits, to turn them into the best they could be. You were a good officer, Detective. I kicked your rear to make sure you made the grade. Now I'm giving you the chance to come back on board. Now I have the chance to right a wrong."

Voynich again stood, shaking each of their hands.

"Thank you, sir," Heart said.

"Oh, don't thank me yet. I'm guessing you're going to be in for one hell of a ride." Voynich turned to Stanton. "Sergeant Stanton, your captain speaks highly of you. That's why I chose you to work with the detective."

"Thank you, sir."

"Keep me informed. Don't forget — every day at seventeen hundred and any time something comes up. Good luck." Voynich returned to his desk. "Dismissed."

Heart and Stanton filed out of the office, silent. After Stanton touched the call button for the elevator, Heart spoke. "Now what?"

"I'll take you to see Cranston."

***

Stanton made the introductions before excusing herself. Once I was alone with Cranston, he pointed to a chair and sat down at his desk as he touched his ear-tab.

"Matthew Heart." Cranston slowly articulated the name. He pivoted in his chair and gestured to a wall display as Heart's information file appeared, replete with statistics, details of time served, and the latest headshot. "The chief informed me he was bringing you in. I read over your file: bad conduct, demotion, dishonorable discharge. Banned from the metrofloat. Yet, for some inexplicable reason, the local police accepted you in the settlements. I would have figured you'd never wear a badge again in your life. Lucky? Or do you have a guardian angel?"

"I thought there was a limit to how much bad luck any one man could have?"

"Your file shows you were given clearance in FS45. That's why you got in."

"Clearance? By whom?"

Cranston touched his ear-tab. "Page thirty-five, paragraph six." He pointed to the wall as the display changed. "Read it yourself."

Heart studied the information, frowning. His file showed his clearance had come from then-inspector Michael Voynich.

"So, you do have a guardian angel," Cranston said.

"I'll be damned," Heart said.

"I assumed you getting chucked out after exemplary service was a bunch of bullshit."

"You should never pick a fight with somebody bigger than you."

"True, but eventually doing somebody wrong comes back to bite you in the ass. And the fact you're here means somebody better look out for theirs."

"I'm here to investigate a murder."

"That's all?" Cranston pushed back in his chair. "Voynich picked you. There are a lot of qualified people here, yet he picks you. He brings in somebody from the outside, so something's going on. Something big."

"I'm the sacrificial lamb. Or the scapegoat. Whatever. I'm dispensable."

"Could be. But it's on orders from Voynich and I doubt he'd be backing the loser." Cranston fiddled with his system. "I've reactivated you. You're free and clear as an upstanding citizen of Metrofloat New York. Try not to piss anybody off."

"Yeah, right."

"I've given you the complete file on Willard Bachmann. Read up on the particulars. Stanton can answer any questions. You know as much as we do and, hopefully, you'll find out what we don't know."

"I've explained why I was supposedly picked," Heart said. "But why Stanton?"

Cranston leaned on one elbow. "My recommendation. She's good. She also needs a break, and I'm hoping this is the personal turnaround for her."

"Personal?"

"Let's say she's like the daughter I never had. She's been through more than any five guys put together, and I'd like to see her successful and happy. Besides, I feel responsible she got into this mess in the first place."

"We talked and she told me a bit, but not much. She's a synth. That unto itself says a lot." Heart eyed Cranston. "It must be quite a story."

"You two are going to work side by side. In fact, your lives will depend on one another. I think it's important to fully understand who your partner is, so I'll tell you what I know — and what she's told me. I don't want to see her hurt again."

Chapter 3

Officer Elizabeth Stanton threw a punch and then turned and kicked. Trooper Jack Balford blocked both moves and backed off, bouncing on the balls of his feet.

"Don't give your opponent an opportunity to think, Stanton." Sergeant Cranston moved around the periphery of the fight area, watching the action. He had been working with the new officer for some time now and knew she had something unique. Cranston pushed her to tap into her inner strength. Buried inside was the confidence that made the difference between an ordinary person and a leader, and Stanton had it. Cranston knew it, but he just had to get her to believe it as well.

Balford feigned a couple of punches and executed a roundhouse. Stanton blocked the kick but stumbled back from the force of the blow.

"Careful," Cranston said.

Stanton punched and followed with a right hook. The trooper defended himself and then came after her with a rain of blows. She staggered back at this onslaught but blocked every punch. Balford smiled, knowing he had the advantage. He twisted his body as he threw a right hook, lowering his other arm to increase force. Stanton deflected the punch and brought her other fist around in a wide arc to his now exposed side. Her glove slammed into his left cheek. Balford staggered several paces to one side and dropped to one knee.

"Okay, that's enough," Cranston said, walking across the mat to join them. "Are you all right, Balford?" Cranston reached down and grabbed the man's left arm.

"Where did that come from?" Balford shook his head, stunned.

Cranston helped the trooper get back up. "That's enough for today. Why don't you two go shower and get ready for ordnance training?" He looked at the clock on the wall. "It's at sixteen hundred. You've got one hour."

"Yes, sir," Stanton said.

Balford rubbed his stinging cheek. "Yes, sir."

Together, they walked off the mat toward the locker room. Cranston smiled as he watched them disappear. He glanced again at the clock.

"Geesh, Stanton," Balford said. "What are you trying to do? Kill me?"

Stanton shrugged. "You drop your guard when you go for your super-duper hook."

"I'll never learn."

"Nope."

At sixteen hundred hours, Cranston walked into the test bay. "Atten-shun!" He stood in front of the five-member squad. "Men, you know the drill. But keep in mind, this is a live drill. We're not fooling around. This isn't a test. This is real. Do your stuff and make me proud."

Cranston walked back and exited as the bay doors slid shut. Ten minutes later, he was standing in the elevated observation area when an explosion shattered the windows with a deafening roar. The force knocked him backward and laid him out on the floor. Stunned, he soon realized sirens were screaming, but his hearing was dulled, indicating his eardrums may have burst. He breathed in smoke, coughing several times. A door opened, and feet stampeded into the room. Muddled voices repeated, "Are you all right?" several times until unseen hands grabbed hold of him and pulled him up.

"Sergeant Cranston, are you okay?"

Disoriented, he looked at the concerned face of a private. "What happened?"

"An explosion, sir. In the bay. We don't know what went wrong." The private turned Cranston toward the door. "Let's get you out of here and down to the infirmary." He began to lead his superior by the arm.

"What about my squad?"

"They're going to the infirmary, sir. But I can't believe anybody survived."

Cranston turned to look out the observation-area windows and stumbled in shock at the destruction below. The private moved to support him, and he righted himself before they walked out.

***

"Hello, Elizabeth."

The male voice sounded calm and soothing. What was that? Was she dreaming? She tried to open her eyes but couldn't complete the simple movement. What was going on? Where was she?

"Elizabeth? Can you hear me?"

She thought to turn her head, but she couldn't feel it. In fact, she couldn't feel anything. What was wrong with her body?

"Hello?" She waited, staring into the darkness. Something was wrong, but clearly somebody was taking care of things. She would be patient and let this person guide her.

"Ah, good. I was worried you couldn't hear me."

"No, I can hear you. Would you tell me where I am?"

"Of course. But first, I would like to introduce myself. I'm Dr. Harvey Osler. Why don't you call me Harvey? I see no reason to be formal."

She listened to the calm tone of his voice. It had a reassuring quality. "Okay, Harvey. Pleased to meet you."

"You've suffered an accident, Elizabeth."

"I figured something must have happened. Since I can't see, I'm convinced you don't have the best of news for me."

"I'm not going to mince words. The news is not good. But I want to give you a chance to adjust."

"Is that why I can't feel my body?"

"Yes."

She remained quiet, pondering the implications of Harvey's answer, and imagined scenarios. Her neck had been broken, and she was now quadriplegic. She had suffered a brain injury that had damaged her senses.

"Elizabeth?"

She came out of her reverie. "Yes, Harvey?"

"I thought I had lost you."

"Sorry. I was going through different reasons that would explain why I can't feel my body. And why I can't see."

"I'll explain everything in due course, but let's move along."

"To give me a chance to adjust."

"Yes."

The voice continued to reassure. She felt she was in good hands, whoever this Harvey was.

"Would you like to see?"

"You can do that?" Were her eyes bandaged? Things might not be as bad as she imagined.

"Yes, I can. Let's move in steps by trying out one thing at a time. I'd hate to fall flat on my face first time out."

She chuckled. "Okay. You're the doctor. But you mean *me* falling flat on *my* face."

"I think of us as being in this together."

"Kind of you."

"Now," Harvey said, "you're going to start to see. Let's go easy."

She stared into the black, feeling a surge of excitement and wondering if there would be a growing brilliance as layer after layer of gauze was removed from her eyes.

"Anything?"

She concentrated. "Nothing."

"Just a moment..." Harvey's voice trailed off as if he was busy doing something.

Her full vision came back, startling her with utter clarity and sharpness. It was as if a switch had been thrown and somebody had turned on a high-definition projection with vibrant colors and superb contrast.

"Oh, Harvey!"

The face of a man came into view. "How are we doing?"

"I can see, but I can't seem to move my eyes."

"Just a second." Harvey's face moved out of view.

After a few moments, her eyes moved, and she turned them left and right and then up and down. "Ah, that's better." Moving her eyes as far to the left as possible, she saw Harvey hunched over a display. "So that's you, Harvey."

The man reappeared in front of her face. "Yes, it's me. I take it your vision is all right?"

"I see quite well. In fact, I'd say better than ever." She swept her eyes around, taking in the room. "This is my hospital room?"

"You could say that."

She looked at Harvey. "Wait. I don't seem to be lying down. I think I'm in an upright position. Am I standing?"

"You're being held upright, so yes, you are, in a sense, standing."

"Doctor?" She continued to stare at Harvey. "What has happened to me?"

He hesitated. "There was an explosion, Elizabeth."

She tried to remember. She could recall her life, her time at the academy, and her training as an officer, but then — nothing.

"You were part of a squad doing a training exercise with live ordnance. Something blew up. The other four members of the squad were killed, but we saved you."

Elizabeth considered what he had just said: everyone dead but her. Bad luck? Good luck? "How badly am I wounded?"

"We recovered your brain."

Elizabeth's gaze darted around. "What does that mean? Where am I?"

A female voice off to one side said, "Doctor, the readings are destabilizing."

Harvey leaned in to look her in the eye. "Elizabeth?"

"Yes, Doctor?"

"I need you to remain calm. Listen to my voice. Concentrate. Go slowly and think carefully. Do not panic. You are in a safe place. I am your friend. Everything's good."

There was a beep behind her head. Harvey's voice was calm and measured. "Elizabeth, listen to me. I'm going to help you, but I need you to help me." There was another beep as Harvey leaned to one side and said, "Benzo, 5 cc."

"Harvey?"

"Yes, Elizabeth?"

"I'm scared."

"That's understandable. But I'm here. And I assure you everything is all right. You have nothing to worry about."

"I can't feel my body because I don't have a body," she said.

"That's right."

"Then... what am I?"

"You're Elizabeth Stanton. You're human. Things are different, but you're still you."

"The benzo must have taken effect. I should be upset, but I'm amused to hear you refer to not having a body as 'different.'" She chuckled. "May I see myself?"

"Are you sure?"

"I must do it eventually. I better get used to this new situation."

"Okay." She watched as he picked up a hand mirror from a table. "Here we go."

She looked at the image in front of her. It was a human-like head. As she looked around, she saw the eyes move. "What am I looking at, Harvey?"

"It's an artificial cranium. This is your new head — the housing for your brain."

"I'm in there. My brain is in there?"

"Yes."

She looked lower and saw the head was sitting on a stand. "I don't have a body."

"You will."

"What do you mean?"

"We're in the process of building you a new body. Everything will be functional — arms and legs. We'll connect the head you now see to a neck, and you will have full range of motion and then some. All of this will be finished off with a lifelike skin so you will look human."

"I remember the rumors. Children talked about cyborgs, but I had never seen one. There was a funny term to describe this: not just a human who wasn't whole, but a human who was no longer human."

"A synth."

She shut her eyes. Gurgling noises came from her voice device.

"Are you all right?"

Elizabeth didn't say anything.

"Don't cry, Elizabeth." Harvey reached out to touch a cheek.

"Am I able to cry? Do I have tear ducts?" Her voice cracked. "My parents weren't whole. I was teased every day as a child about my parents not being the same as everybody else. Even though I was whole, I was made to feel as if I wasn't, as if I was different, as if I was inferior." She opened her eyes and looked at Harvey. "Now I truly am different. I haven't lost an arm or a leg. I've lost everything." She shut her eyes again. "Oh, Harvey!"

"Science has made great strides, Elizabeth." Harvey's voice sounded comforting. "You may have lost your body, but you didn't lose your life. You can still live a full one. Granted, it will not be the same as before, but you have a chance. And don't forget the other four members of your squad didn't get that chance."

She remained silent.

"It's going to be an adventure. It's a chance to go where few have gone before." Harvey's voice now had a hopeful timbre. "What do you say? Are you with me? Shall we give this a go?"

Elizabeth opened her eyes and looked at him. "I have little choice. But I appreciate your enthusiasm."

"I'm here to help. I'm here to inspire." Harvey motioned to one side. "If you don't mind, there's somebody who would like to see you."

She turned her eyes, but whoever was there stood out of her field of view. She heard a door open and saw somebody walk in from the left.

"Hello, Officer." Sergeant Cranston came into sight.

"Sir," she said.

"You seem in good hands."

"I guess. I'm not yet sure what's going on."

"You're lucky to be alive."

"So I've been told. But, despite what the doctor says, I'm not sure what the future holds for me."

"You'll be back."

"Sir?"

"You'll be back. You'll be back to duty."

"With all due respect, sir..."

"I've seen it."

"Pardon?"

Cranston gave a knowing nod. "I've seen it, Stanton. You're not the first. I've worked with artificial humans, cyborgs. We're used to the idea of prosths: an artificial arm or leg or even an organ. What's the next step? Everything. The science is there. It's a question of pushing the idea to its ultimate conclusion by replacing every limb and organ. The essential part, the essence of any human, is their brain. Everything else can be replaced, and you still have the same person. What's an arm but a device, a tool, to carry out specific tasks? It doesn't matter what tool you use, but it does matter what you do with it. That's where the brain comes in — the person."

"But—"

"Elizabeth?" Cranston leaned closer.

"Yes?"

"You and I go back."

"Yes, sir."

"You and I share a common history. Our families have suffered the ignominy of not being whole and being rejected by our peers. Nothing in the city is worse than being ostracized."

"Yes."

"I want you to rise above it. You can be better than that, better than them. Prove to the world Elizabeth Stanton is still Elizabeth Stanton."

She stared at him, trying to grasp the task ahead of her.

"You have a unique opportunity to come back. And you

can come back in a way that is better than before." Cranston stood up straight. "Officer Stanton?"

"Yes, sir?"

"Make me proud. I expect you back on active duty."

"Really, sir?"

"Yes. And that's an order." Cranston turned and walked away.

Harvey came back into view. "Your commander has a lot of confidence in you."

"So it seems."

"And he gave you an order."

"I can't ignore that."

"No, you can't." He examined a display off to one side. "Elizabeth?"

"Yes?"

"My crew will now be coming in to assemble your body. We'll be going through a regimen of therapeutic training to familiarize your neural pathways with your new organs and limbs. While the machine–human interface is seamless, replacing an entire body can be confusing for the brain. An artificial body may not react like a real one, and we need to discover and adjust for those differences."

"Doctor?"

"Yes?"

"I'm never going to be the same."

Harvey grinned. "Elizabeth, I think you'll be surprised. The latest innovations in prosthetics have brought the amalgamation of human and machine to a level of such seamlessness, only the experts can tell the difference by sight. Your average person often remains unaware of any artificial limbs."

"But a cyborg, a synth — it's not a limb; it's the entire person."

"Same thing, but on a grander scale."

Out of sight, a door opened and there was the sound of wheels moving across the floor. "Ah, gentlemen," Harvey said. "Let's get everything set up. Our patient is awake and ready to go."

She watched as several men wheeled in a support carriage containing various human parts. She counted two legs and two arms among other things she didn't recognize. They worked around her, out of sight. Elizabeth strained but could only turn her eyes so far. So she gave up and stared at the other side of the room. Harvey spoke to the men several times while moving in and out of her field of vision. She felt a growing sense of anticipation and thought that Harvey was right after all. This was an adventure, and she should accept it as it came. The alternative was being dead.

"Elizabeth?"

"Yes, Harvey."

"I want to run you through a series of tests, so we can calibrate the BCI–prosthesis interaction."

"I beg your pardon?"

Harvey chuckled. "Sorry, I'm getting technical. *BCI* is brain–computer interface, which dictates how your brain interacts with the various components governing your body. When you think of moving your arm, we want to make sure the interface corresponds to how your brain works. If you think of grabbing hold of something, we want you to have a reasonable grip, not one that's strong enough to crush the item."

As Elizabeth continued to stare forward, Harvey stepped into view and fiddled with something around her neck. After a moment, he stepped back. "Okay, I want you to turn your head to the left."

Elizabeth turned her head sideways, curious about what to expect.

"You're not as restricted as a normal human being, Elizabeth."

"What do you mean?"

"Try turning your head again, but this time don't stop. You can turn a full hundred-and-eighty degrees."

"Really?" She again rotated her head to the left, stopping at ninety degrees. "Here goes." She continued until her head sat backward. "Oh, this is weird!"

"Don't forget that we can, in some ways, improve the human body: greater mobility, greater strength, and greater speed. I'm aware of the value our culture puts on being whole, but as your Sergeant Cranston said, the essence of a human being is the brain, not the body."

She returned her head to the forward position and then turned it one-hundred-and-eighty degrees to the right. "I don't remember how far I could rotate my head before."

"An average human can rotate their head about eighty degrees."

"That's all?"

"That's it." Harvey looked at a display. "Let's try your limbs. How about you try raising your right arm? But go slowly. We need to calibrate the movement to your somatic nervous system."

"My what?"

"Sorry, technical jargon. It's the part of your nervous system that deals with voluntary movements such as your arms and legs. We have to adjust the BCI to your unique thinking." Harvey pointed to her right arm. "Go ahead. Try it."

Elizabeth looked down and watched her arm move upward until it was straight out from her shoulder. "How's that?"

"Good. Now move it to the side."

Her arm spun to the right and slammed into something solid. She whipped her head around in time to see a display monitor atop a pole topple over. A hand reached over and grabbed the metal stand.

"Oops!" Harvey said, righting the monitor and moving it out of the way. "That's what I mean by needing to calibrate your body. Sometimes what you think of as a regular movement, the BCI interprets as a signal to move quickly in that direction."

"Sorry."

"No problem. I'll make adjustments. Everybody is unique, and the BCI must be attuned to the individual. But let me be clear — there will be a learning process on your part. An artificial limb isn't like a real limb, and you will find you have to learn how to move it in the same way."

"Okay."

"As I said, we have augmented the human body, but you must learn to control it."

"Greater strength?"

"You are several times stronger than a normal human being."

"What does that mean, exactly?"

"A prosth can increase a limb's strength and speed, but the overall effect is restricted by the human body. A chain is only as strong as its weakest link. Even if a limb can lift a great weight, the rest of the body can't support it. You, however, have every part replaced, so the cumulative effect is considerable." Harvey smiled. "You may be giving up something, but you're also getting something. It's going to take time to learn to deal with this new range of strength and movement. You must learn to shake hands without crushing the other person's hand and use a touchscreen without punching a hole in the display. You have power, but you must control it and use it wisely."

***

Harvey worked methodically with Elizabeth. She learned how to walk, how to sit, and how to move in general — things she had done so naturally when she was whole. She had to start all over again, but, as Cranston had said, this was an opportunity to come back when others had not been so lucky. What had Harvey called it? An adventure. The more she worked things through, the more she was at ease with herself and her new body. She wasn't physically whole, but she was still somebody. She was still alive. And she still had a chance.

Several months later, Elizabeth stared at herself in the mirror of the ladies' room. She had visited a salon and got her latest wig coiffed. The attendant had also helped with her makeup, and Elizabeth thought she looked good. One stylish dress later, she was impressed; she felt like a woman. But something still nagged her.

Since her accident, Elizabeth had shied away from people. As she'd feared, she was called, by some, a freak, so why run the risk of people rebuffing her and humiliating herself? However, during her retraining and reintegration into the service, she had developed some camaraderie with her fellow officers and had even gone so far as to accept their invitations for after-work drinks, several times. During these moments of chatting and sharing a few laughs, she had felt a sense of normalcy. She wasn't different; she was like everybody else.

Two days earlier, after a round of drinks, Elizabeth had left the bar at the same time as one of her colleagues. Once outside, Marty said the usual, "See you tomorrow" but didn't walk away. He hesitated. She was wondering what else Marty had to say when he leaned in and kissed her on the cheek. Then he left.

She had raised her hand and touched her cheek, shocked. When she was whole she had had relations, and had even once had a long-term boyfriend. But, since the accident, she figured that part of her life was over. No man would want a synth. No man would want a fake woman. She had never once considered the possibility of ever having a normal relationship again.

And now? Marty had kissed her. Okay, he had kissed her on the cheek, but he had still kissed her. Her heart was aflutter at recalling the memory, and she beamed at herself in the mirror. Technically, she didn't have a heart, but could she say her cardio-assist regulatory system skipped a beat? Was the autonomic part of her brain triggering her synth body to release hormones like dopamine or oxytocin? Whatever the case, Elizabeth felt something she had not felt in a long time — something she thought she would never feel again.

Elizabeth left the ladies' room and walked along the elevated perimeter of the bar. Below, she saw the table where Marty and the rest of her colleagues were boisterously laughing. As she passed a nearby pillar, she heard someone say,

"You kissed her? You kissed a synth?" The man snorted, and she quickly retreated behind the support.

"It was a unique opportunity," Marty said.

Another voice chimed in. "I can't imagine doing it with a robot."

Marty chuckled. "Don't knock it if you haven't tried it."

"Sorry, I'll stick with a whole."

"Anybody can have a whole. I want to get me a synth."

Elizabeth peeked around the pillar and saw Marty sitting with his hands behind his head, grinning at the others. Without another thought, she took a half step to the railing and leaned over. She grabbed Marty by the left wrist and lifted. Everyone at the table gasped. Pulling him out of the seat, she held him high enough so their eyes were level. He stared back, stunned, his legs dangling just above the table.

"It's a unique opportunity to do it with a robot," Elizabeth said, sarcastically. "You'll be a hero." She let go of him. Marty dropped to the floor and fell over, pushing his chair to one side and crashing into the man sitting beside him. Elizabeth glared at the group and they all stared back, their mouths agape. Without another word, she stood back up and stomped to the exit, yanking open the door so hard she tore the handle out of its base.

Alone at home, Elizabeth cried, but she had no tears. Her artificial eyes were self-lubricating, and she had no tear ducts. Her sobs gave way to ironic chuckles. It hurt, but it was absurd. She should have realized it was too good to be true. Hope had led her astray. She was a synth, a freak. No man would want her in the way she needed. She wasn't whole. She wasn't even human. Her fellow officers had proved she'd been right all along, and she vowed never to let such a thing happen again. It was embarrassing. It was humiliating. She had to accept she was no longer a woman.

Elizabeth Stanton, soldier. Elizabeth Stanton, police officer. Elizabeth Stanton, former human being.

Chapter 4

Heart stood at the one-way mirror with Stanton, looking at the two teenage boys.

"Our first witnesses to the crime," Stanton said. "Alan Sharp, eighteen, and Terry Bradley, seventeen. The two of them bypassed security at AG Station Twelve and were bungee jumping over FS45 when Bachmann was killed."

"Really?"

"As with all kids, there's notoriety that comes with doing crazy stunts. An underground group of jumpers likes to drop over the settlements and pick up recognizable souvenirs, like signs, as proof of their derring-do. I wouldn't be surprised if Alan and Terry have something from FS45 up on the walls of their bedrooms."

"Bungee. Hmph. I wonder if they'll ever make personalized AG in backpacks."

"I've seen military prototypes. They're large, unwieldy, and costly. I don't see it anytime soon."

Heart nodded.

"I'll do the talking." Stanton opened the door to Interrogation Room #5, and they sat down in front of the two boys.

"Good evening, gentlemen," Stanton said as she laid a hand-tab on the table. "We'd like to ask you a few questions."

Alan leaned back and hooked his left arm on the back of the chair. "I want to see a lawyer."

Stanton touched the hand-tab. "Why? Do something wrong?"

"I've got rights."

"Yes, you have rights. The right to remain silent. The right to an attorney. But I'm not charging you with anything. I want to know what you saw last night."

"Well—" Terry said.

Alan swatted his friend's arm. "Shut up, Terry." He smirked at Stanton.

"Mr. Sharp." Stanton smiled. "You bypassed security to

gain entrance to Antigrav Station Twelve. That is a summary offense, punishable by both a fine and up to a year in prison. You used unauthorized equipment on the catwalk — your bungee system — which is punishable by a fine of up to a thousand credits. You illegally threw something off the metrofloat, yourself, which is also punishable by a fine and a prison sentence. Let's see..." Stanton glanced at the hand-tab. "You now owe me two years in jail and twelve thousand credits."

Alan squinted. "Listen, lady—"

Stanton slammed her fist down on the metal tabletop with a loud bang. The two boys jumped in their seats and stared at her as she moved her hand to one side to reveal an indentation in the shape of her fist. "The name is Sergeant Stanton. You will address me by my rank and name, or with ma'am." She glared at them. "What did you see last night?"

Terry turned to look at his friend. Alan stared at the indentation. The rest of the interview passed without incident. Both boys talked in detail, but Alan had more to say, as the designated jumper. Stanton thanked them after. "You're free to go. If we have any further questions, we'll be in contact."

After the boys left, Stanton picked up the hand-tab. "Not much to that, but we had to ask."

Heart ran his hand over the indentation. "Remind me not to piss you off."

"Let's go visit the crime scene."

***

Imperial Towers was an exclusive residential property on the edge of the city — high-class, luxurious, and expensive. Those with an outside condo had an uninterrupted view away from the city, down and out over the ground. Bachmann's suite comprised the top floor, which Heart wasn't surprised to discover. Top story for the top guy — or the formerly soon-to-be top guy.

On the front door hung a police sign, and Stanton had to

give a thumbprint on a special security lock to gain entrance. "We're here at twenty hours after the crime."

"Forensics was that precise?" Heart strolled into the center of the living room and looked around.

"Right to the minute life ended. Plus, we know when the ID stopped. The two events are fifteen minutes apart."

"What security systems are in place?"

"The usual, but there doesn't seem to be a record of any activity."

"You mean nothing bad going on."

"No, I mean no activity at all."

Heart frowned. "Somebody disabled security?"

"We're not yet sure."

"What about access to the building?"

"So far, all chip access is accounted for."

"Could somebody get in without a chip?"

Stanton smirked. "It's illegal for anyone not to be chipped, but there are ways of fooling ID systems: Person A comes in, but the system records Person B."

"Somebody could have come in from above."

"True. We wondered about that. And we also wondered if said person, or persons, had the means of taking out the security system. There are redundancies built into the system, but no matter how secure you make it, somebody will eventually figure out how to bust in."

Heart pivoted slowly in the center of the room. "Several weapon discharges."

"Yes."

"Anything else?"

"Investigators determined wrist restraints were used on that chair. We're guessing the victim was held in place while the cerebral extraction took place."

Heart looked at the chair Stanton had indicated. "Nobody will ever know what Bachmann knew."

"That's right. We can't data-mine the visual memory for the identity of the killer, and whatever secrets he had are gone, too. It's curious. Somebody didn't just want to stop Bachmann —

they also wanted to make sure nobody else could carry on his work."

"I'll give them an A for determination and thoroughness."

Stanton walked to the terrace door and opened it. "Follow me."

They strolled around, ending up on the far side. She pointed over the barrier. "We assume it's from here the body was dumped."

Heart leaned over and looked down. In the twilight he could see the ground was over a kilometer below. A few lights twinkled here and there.

"Fifty stories to the city streets. Another klick to the ground."

"That's quite the drop. No wonder the body ended up as it did."

"I'm not sure why it was necessary to drop the body over the side," Stanton said. "Extracting the brain was more than enough to stop us from gaining access to the man's memories. Pulverizing the dead body is a statement."

"Yes." Heart turned back to the terrace, eying the railing around the perimeter. "Any idea on how the culprit got up here?"

"I'm sure it was a flivver."

"Any access from one of the neighboring buildings?"

"There are connecting walkways for this building at the twentieth, thirtieth, and fortieth levels. Nothing this high. The fiftieth and last story is Bachmann's private condo. It is a special and exclusive address."

Heart stopped and looked out at the other buildings, studying the lights of the apartments and peering into various windows. "I've always found it interesting to peek into windows like this."

Stanton gave him a sidelong glance.

"Nothing perverted. It can sometimes be mesmerizing to watch somebody who's unaware they're being watched. You get to see the real person. No artifice." Heart stared at the adjacent building, scanning another level. He stopped and looked back. "What's that?"

"What's what?" Stanton moved against the railing and followed the length of his arm to where he was pointing.

"Across the way, two levels down from where we are, I can just see something against the building. Do these buildings have flivver parking at upper levels?"

"Not that I know of." Stanton leaned over the railing to get a better view.

Heart touched his ear-tab and his eye display came out. "Telescopic," he instructed, looking into the darkness. "Zoom in, night enhancement." He pointed again. "Do you see it? There's a flivver parked against that building at the forty-eighth level."

"Yes," she said. "I'm imaging and requesting identification."

"I don't detect any transponder."

"That's worth taking a look at. Never mind it being illegal; it makes you think somebody has something to hide." Her voice changed. "Officer Stanton, Badge #4711. Request Patrol Investigation, Imperial Towers. Adjacent building, north, forty-eighth level. There is an unmarked flivver parked alongside the building. No transponder." She was quiet and then said, "Copy."

As they stood staring at the car, it moved. They watched it pass by several lighted windows until it came to the end of the building, where it turned the corner and disappeared.

"I think the driver was listening to us," Heart said. "Are we being spied on?"

"Anything is possible." Stanton spoke again, "Officer Stanton, Badge #4711. Tell Patrol Investigation to look for any flivvers at the upper levels of all buildings adjacent to Imperial Towers." She listened. "Copy."

"Now what?"

"It's late. Let's call it a day."

"Okay, I'll head home. Where can I pick up an autocab?"

"I'll take you downstairs and get you set up."

***

Heart gave his FS45 coordinates, and the autocab took over. He settled into one of the four pivoting seats, watching the metrofloat recede in the distance. It would be a half-hour ride back to the settlement — an uneventful journey over the vast farmlands below.

Heart called up the display screen from the armrest and sampled the available entertainment. Nothing caught his eye, so he turned off the display and looked out at the darkness in various directions. He saw the occasional light of a crossroad below — a way station for those working far from home.

A moving light appeared suddenly from behind. Heart pushed his face against the window. Unable to see anything, he shifted in his seat and stared out the back window. At first there was nothing, but then he realized running lights were coming up behind the autocab. They were dim and difficult to see. Heart had not expected any traffic out here and couldn't imagine who would be going to the settlement at this hour.

The other flivver pulled up alongside the autocab. Heart again rotated his seat and tried to discern who was in the other car. He noticed its side window was open just as a blue spark shot out. Every light in the autocab blacked out, and the vehicle took a nosedive. Heart rose out of his seat as the car free-fell, panicking when he realized the flivver had lost all power and was now plummeting to the ground. From the height of a kilometer, he knew he had less than fifteen seconds to make his escape.

Heart pulled himself into the seat and, with a practiced movement, slipped on both emergency shoulder straps, buckling them tight. He reached down to his left and yanked up on a release lever. The roof of the autocab disappeared, and explosive bolts hurled the seat out of the car. The wind whipped past as Heart tumbled several times through the darkness. A pop was followed by a rustling noise as a parachute deployed overhead. There was a sharp jerk, and his rapid fall slowed to a gentle descent.

His heart pounded in his ears. After a few seconds, the disabled autocab crashed close by with a crunch of metal and glass. Heart gaped into the darkness. The lights on the underside of his seat shone downward, but he could see nothing to discern how far he was from the ground. He was in the middle of a nerve-racking void.

He landed with a thump, the spring-loaded seat base absorbing the shock. After the seat had teetered and fallen over, Heart popped the buckle and rolled free. There was no wind, and the parachute settled on the ground.

Heart stood and brushed himself off. He looked up at the sky but saw no trace of the other flivver. Taking several deep breaths, he tried to calm himself but his hands shook. Somebody had tried to kill him.

Heart pressed his ear-tab and called up communications, speaking with Dispatch about his situation. They said a car would be out there in fifteen minutes. He glanced at the seat and noticed a flashing light on the back. The transponder would have notified the cab company of a problem, and Heart figured they would soon be out here to investigate. A crash would also involve the police, so he'd have some company.

It was dead quiet. Heart stood in the middle of a vast field. Only the stars in the clear sky provided any light, as the moon had not yet risen. Righting the seat, he sat down, thinking he might as well be comfortable while he waited.

A patrol from FS45 arrived, as promised, in fifteen minutes. Ten minutes later the MetPol showed up, followed by a rep from the cab company. They set up a spotlight so they could view the crashed car, and Heart repeated his story several times. He knew they would verify transponder logs, check flight plans, and investigate any activity in the area. Would anything come of it? Heart had his doubts. Whoever was behind this knew what they were doing. If they could get into Bachmann's condo unannounced and leave without a trace, they could bypass any flight records showing them anywhere near his cab.

Heart's day had started with a hangover. It ended with an

attempt on his life.

***

The patrol dropped him off at the Low Cost Lodge. On the way to his suite, he noticed the door to Sally's place was propped open. Curious, he knocked and heard footsteps.

The door swung open to reveal a voluptuous woman, cascades of blond hair falling over her shoulders. "Hey, Matty." She beamed. "I was hoping you'd stop by."

"You're up late, Christine."

"Catching up on work," she said, retying her bathrobe. "Come on in. Can I get you anything?"

"Oddly enough, I wouldn't mind a glass of water."

"Sure. Have a seat." She got out a glass and busied herself at the refrigerator. "I wanted to thank you for helping Sally this afternoon."

"No problem. I'm glad to oblige."

Setting the glass on the kitchen table, she leaned over to kiss him on the mouth. "My Prince Charming."

Heart chuckled.

Christine sat and crossed her legs, causing the robe to fall open. "Oops." She pulled the two sides together and covered her exposed thigh.

"Please, no need to stand on ceremony for me." He pulled each side of the robe away to reveal her legs. "I want you to be comfortable."

"Really, now." She smirked. "You always make me feel like a woman."

His gaze fell upon an e-pamph on the far side of the table. "What's that?"

"Oh, I don't know. Idle thoughts."

He held the e-pamph in his hand. "Arti-vag? Are you going to continue your transition?"

"It's a tough decision."

"Why? You've always wanted to do it."

"There's always been the question of the cost. I never had

enough credits."

"I've offered to help."

"You're a generous man, Matty. You've been kind to Sally and me. But I need to be independent. It's a tough world out there."

Heart slid his finger across the surface and flipped through the pages, pulling the pamphlet closer to study the text. "This says it has built-in vibration functions. Really?"

"I talked with one of the workers at the brothel. Jessica got one a year ago, and she's become popular with the clients. It's easier to keep clean; easier to avoid infections."

He scratched his forehead, wondering about the implications.

"Who knows? I could take a second job." She chuckled.

"I told you I can get you a job interview at the precinct."

"That's nice of you, but I enjoy working for the farmers' union. I like to do what I can to help others in the community."

"My offer stands, Chris. I'll help if you let me."

"I appreciate it, Matty." She caressed his forearm. "I've wondered if I should keep both."

"Both? Why both?"

"I've always felt I was really a woman. I've always known that. But that doesn't mean I haven't enjoyed playing with the equipment. Besides, how many men enjoy a woman with a little extra?"

Heart grinned as he flipped to the next page.

"How funny," she continued, "to start out as Sally's father and end up as her mother. If Lili hadn't died, would I have continued my transition?"

"I think you would have."

"Yeah, you're right. And lucky Sally would have ended up with two mothers." She sighed. "So horrible to lose Lili."

"Necrofasc shows no mercy."

"I don't know how I would have survived without Sally. Oh, Matty, she means everything to me. She gives me the strength to carry on."

"You do love your daughter."

"God, do I ever." Christine glanced at the time. "It's coming up to midnight. Do you want to watch the news together?"

"Sure."

"Give me a moment. I'd like to finish changing."

Heart continued to browse the e-pamph, glancing into the bedroom where she had disappeared. He watched as Christine put one foot on the bed and fiddled with something at the top of her thigh, using both hands to strip away the arti-flesh and expose her mechanical limb. With the distinct step-click of the metal foot on the hard floor, she walked to a dresser. "I hope you don't mind, but I find the arti-flesh sometimes chafes my stump. I like to leave it off for a while."

"You don't have to dress up on my account. I like you as you are."

"You're sweet. The public isn't so forgiving."

"I appreciate the wrapping as much as the next person, but I love what's inside."

Christine laughed as she leaned into a mirror and worked her fingertips into the top of her forehead. She pulled the hair away and peeled off the flesh from the right side of her head.

"Two minutes to the news."

"Coming." She arranged the hair and flesh on top of the dresser and strode out from the bedroom. Step-click. "Me, *au naturel.*"

Heart looked up. Her mechanical right eye was rotating continuously. "Are you all right?"

"What?"

"Your eye."

"Oh, shoot." Christine slapped the side of her head and the eye stopped moving. "I must go in for servicing. This stupid thing acted up about a week ago, too. It doesn't do it all the time, but every once in a while I look like I'm stoned out of my mind. I've freaked out a few people."

He snorted. "Let's go."

Moving to the living room, they sat on the couch. Heart

pulled out his ear-tab but Christine put her hand on his.

"I'll do it. One nice thing about the arti-eye is that the basic model comes with remote-device control. Too bad I couldn't afford the full-blown communicator model, but this is better than nothing." The wall screen lit up. "We have to keep the sound down. I don't want to wake Sally."

"I'll put on my ear-tab, and then we can keep the sound off."

"Good idea." She brought both her human and mechanical legs onto the couch, curling up against him. Heart wrapped his left arm around her shoulders and kissed the metal of her exposed head plate. "You're cuddly tonight."

"I enjoy being hugged. I feel safe and protected."

He leaned his head against hers, and they watched the news in silence.

***

Heart woke with a start. Glancing at the display, he realized he'd been asleep for an hour. Christine was gone. He yawned and stretched his arms. An e-sheet on the table read, "You're welcome anytime."

He tiptoed to the bedroom door. In the semi-darkness he could just make out the curve of Christine's body beneath the sheet. He checked the time and sighed. Taking a last look at the sleeping figure, he shut the door.

On the e-sheet, he wrote, "Work. Early. I hate being a responsible adult."

It was then he noticed Sally standing outside the door to her bedroom.

"What are you doing up?" he asked.

"I had to go to the bathroom."

"We shouldn't drink before bed."

"Tuck me in, Matty."

"Okay." He followed her into the room. She slipped in between the covers as he pushed a loose end under the mattress and sat on the edge. "Are you going back to sleep?"

"I guess." Part of her face was visible in the light from the living room.

"How's Mom's new boyfriend?"

"He's okay. He treats Mom well, and he's nice to me."

"That sounds like a good thing."

"Why didn't you marry Mom?"

"We talked about it, but your mother is a stubborn woman. She wants to do things on her own. Plus, she says I don't belong here — I'm a city boy and, eventually, I'll end up going back there."

"I wish you were my daddy."

He smiled at her in the dim glow. "You and I will always be friends."

"Promise?"

"I promise." He leaned over and kissed Sally's forehead. "Good night," he said as he paused at the door and smiled back at her.

"Good night, Matty."

He turned off the display and eased the door shut as he left the suite.

Chapter 5

Something cold and metallic prodded his cheek. Heart froze, staring at the forkful of Wang's breakfast he held in front of his open mouth. A familiar male voice sneered at him. "You can't keep a good man down, now, can you, Mister A-hole?"

Heart turned his head, pushing it against the barrel of a gun. He looked up to see the big brother of the running-blade thief.

"This time I came back with reinforcements. Now you don't have the advantage."

Three armed men stood behind Heart's assailant. One of them was pointing a gun at Wang.

"The good guy will not come to your rescue this time." The man jabbed the gun into Heart's cheek. "I think I should blow a hole in your head. Mister Tough Guy isn't so tough when he's all by himself."

Heart looked the big guy in the eye. "Wang?"

"Yes?"

"You better sit down."

"Aw jeez, you're not going to do that?"

The big guy frowned, looking at Wang and then back at Heart. He poked Heart's cheek with the gun. "I'm in command here, and I'll do the talking. You sit there and keep your mouth shut."

Heart pivoted. In one continuous motion, he swept the barrel of the gun away with one hand as he brought the other into his jacket. This startled the big guy, and he pulled the trigger. A blue arc discharged, cracking against a display case behind the counter and blowing out the glass front. Heart raised his left foot and kicked into the man's thigh. As he twisted, Heart took his hand from his jacket and tossed a disk into the air in front of him. There was a blinding flash, followed by a loud bang. The big guy and two others fell to the ground, while the fourth stomped about, cursing, as his arms flopped uselessly at his sides.

The big guy tried to get up but discovered his mechanical

legs no longer functioned. "You bastard." He rolled over and used his human arm to take aim at Heart.

Heart touched his ear-tab. "Officer Heart at Wang's Food Bar. Four to pick up." The big guy pulled the trigger several times before giving up, gawking at his now useless gun.

Heart turned back to the counter and took a bite of cricket. "How long?" Wang said.

"They'll do a reset as soon as they get here. Ten minutes."

"Why can't I do a reset?"

"My stun disk engages the security lock, and only the cops have the code for a police-authorized lockout."

The big guy threw his gun, grazing Heart's leg. "You bastard!"

Heart held up a forkful of food. "Hey, Wang."

"What?" Wang sat, his prosth arms inactive and hanging at his sides.

"Delicious."

"Can't you guys figure out how to make that stunner work selectively?"

Heart grunted as he ate.

"Why can't you do a reset?"

"That's the job of the arrest van."

"With friends like you..."

Heart took a sip of Yerba.

A few minutes later, two officers manhandled the big guy and his three cronies into the arrest van. The driver had had to first reset their prosths so they could walk, before taking care of Wang.

"I'll pay up, Wang," Heart said.

"And don't forget the tip."

"Twenty percent."

"Thirty."

Heart bit his lip. "Thirty?"

"How about the inconvenience of not being able to move for twenty minutes?" Wang clicked his tongue. "You and your hotshot stun bullshit."

Heart sighed as he touched the screen of the POS and then

set out for the precinct.

Stanton answered his call. "You've been gone a mere twelve hours and you've already run into trouble."

"I lead a charmed life."

"Somebody isn't wasting any time. Voynich warned us."

"Last night, I checked all registered flights between Metrofloat and the settlement. There were none, other than my autocab. Did you check flivvers in the vicinity of Imperial Towers?"

"Nothing."

"We're being watched, but we're being watched by somebody able to work off the grid."

"Do you have a plan?"

"I'd like to interview each of the remaining four members of the OligCouncil. Can you set it up?"

"Normally, I'd say a lowly detective would have little chance of seeing any of them, but your newfound clout will open doors. Voynich will help."

"See you in an hour."

***

Heart looked at Stanton's uniform. "I don't remember the last time I had clothes that neat and pressed."

"This is the way we do things here on the 'float."

"Money, power, privilege. Things are dustier on the ground."

"First up," Stanton said, "Dhatri Singh. Elder statesman, the longest-standing member of the council, and the richest man on the 'float. His secretary says we can have fifteen minutes."

The police flivver docked at the seventy-third floor — the upper aerial foyer. Stanton and Heart exited the vehicle and took an elevator to the eightieth floor, where they announced their arrival to a secretary. "Sergeant Stanton and Detective Heart to see Mr. Singh."

"One moment." The secretary touched her ear-tab and her

display moved into position. "That's odd. He's not answering. He may be preoccupied." She touched the ear-tab again as she got up from her desk. "If you will give me a moment." She disappeared through a door.

They stood at the reception counter, idly looking around, when there came a loud scream. Bolting around the desk, Heart pushed the door open, and he and Stanton burst into the room. The secretary was standing off to one side, her hands held to her face, staring in horror at the chair behind a large desk. There was a man's body sitting in it but it had no head.

"The chair was backward, and I couldn't see him. I called out, but he didn't answer." The woman wept periodically. "I grabbed the back of the chair and turned it around. Oh my God!"

Heart examined the body.

"Did anybody else enter or exit the office today?" Stanton moved to the woman and watched her closely.

"Nobody." The receptionist was now sobbing and wiped her nose with the back of her hand. "Mr. Singh went into his office at nine thirty, saying he would be tied up in conference calls. I spoke to him when you called an hour later, and he said he could spare you fifteen minutes at eleven thirty. That's the last time I saw him."

"You actually saw him?"

"Yes. No. Well, I saw him via the display. I didn't go into his office. We communicated via the interoffice chat, and then he called me and I spoke to him via video."

Heart moved back from the body. "Curious."

Stanton turned to him. "What?"

"He's been shot in the chest. That would have been enough to kill him, but the perpetrator also took his head. Why?"

"The same as with Bachmann. So we can't reconstruct his memories."

"But what did Bachmann and Singh see that the killer doesn't want us to know?"

"The face of the killer?"

"There are a lot of ways to kill someone without them

seeing your face." Heart looked at the woman. "Miss?"

"Yes?"

"What's your name?"

"Katie Rathmann." Her voice wavered from terror.

"Do you have any security recordings of this office?"

"No. In fact, Mr. Singh had the office swept once a month for bugs."

"He did?"

"Yes. He was paranoid, but he was meticulous in his paranoia. Then again, you don't get to the top of the ladder without being worried about your enemies."

"He had a lot?"

Katie shrugged. "He is, or he was, the richest man in Metrofloat New York. That can make enemies: the jealous, the hangers-on, the greedy."

Heart nodded. "Call it in, Sergeant."

Stanton moved to one side, pressed her ear-tab, and reported to Central.

Heart stepped toward Katie. "What do you know of Willard Bachmann?"

"The usual: next in line for the OligCouncil, head of the Big Five. Not the richest, but the most ambitious."

Stanton walked back to where Heart and the secretary stood. "Forensics will be here in fifteen. I'm betting, though, they won't find anything."

Heart turned to Katie. "I'd like you to go back to your desk and wait, please. A team of police will arrive shortly, and they'll want to take a full statement from you."

"All right." Katie backed away, her eyes fixed on the body until she turned and disappeared out the door.

"Two down, three to go," Heart said.

Stanton walked over to the body. "You think whoever did this is going after the entire council?"

"It's a possibility. This is more than a coincidence."

"I suppose killing is the age-old method of wresting power."

"You can't argue with success."

"We need to call Voynich. I'm sure he'll want to put protection on the remaining three members of the council." Stanton examined the chest and neck of the body. "No blood. Whoever removed the head cauterized the flesh, so there was no bleeding."

"Neat and tidy. However, the shot would have stopped the heart, so it was no longer pumping."

"No oozing either."

Heart pulled out his communicator and touched the screen. He held it to his ear and waited. "We have an update." Heart glanced at Stanton. "I'll put you on speaker."

Voynich's voice boomed from the device. "What's the update?"

"Dhatri Singh is dead."

There was silence.

"Did you hear me?"

"Yes," Voynich said.

"The perpetrator used the same method as with Bachmann. However, this time they didn't just take the brain. I'm looking at the decapitated body right now. Stanton has called in a forensics team. There will more than likely be nothing to go on. We recommend protection for the remaining three members of the council, but..."

"Go on."

"I'm wondering, which of the remaining three is the culprit? If this is a power grab, and killing your rivals is the preferred method, it stands to reason one of the three will kill the other two."

"I'll take care of the protection. You two keep digging. I understand you have visits planned for all three today."

"Yes, sir."

"Keep me updated. Voynich out."

Heart put the device back in his pocket. "How did the perp get in and out?" He turned, studying the room.

Stanton watched him. "I'm assuming this person was able to override any security."

"You heard Katie. No recording devices in this room."

"Access to the floor: elevators, stairwells."

Heart looked toward the windows. "What about outside the building?"

"There are traffic monitors, but they can be overridden too."

"Does 'overridden' mean that the recording is blank?"

"Of course," Stanton said. "Are you thinking of altering an image? As in removing something?"

"Yes."

"As far as I know, you can do that after the fact with a special process. You can't modify a camera to not record something. You can only turn a camera off."

Heart walked to a window and looked at the middle seam between two panels. "The frame has a scratch on it."

"Where?"

"Here. Midlevel. At the height where somebody crouching and carrying something might accidentally hit the edge."

Stanton walked over and inspected the window.

"You said you didn't find anything about a flivver at Imperial Towers," he said.

"That's right."

"What did you check?"

"Traffic cams."

"You have cams this high up?"

"There are authorized flivver corridors at various levels. Driving outside those zones requires a special permit. People can't just wander around or we'd have chaos in the air."

"My guess is the person who did this came in through the window and went back out the same way. Let's have Forensics look outside for any marks. Maybe a chip in the paint. The flivver might have bumped the building and scratched its side. The weight of a human being getting in and out of the vehicle destabilizes its float."

"Do we put out an APB for a scratched flivver?"

"Okay, it's not much to go on, but we do have to look at everything. Who knows where any of this will lead?"

"Sergeant Stanton?"

They turned to the door. A woman and two men stood at the entrance, surveying the scene.

"Please, come in and get started." Stanton walked into the middle of the room and gestured to the chair. "That is — that was Dhatri Singh. I'll fill you in on what we know."

Heart re-examined the window and the lock. Looking out the window, he checked left and right and then up and down. Something caught his eye. He touched his ear-tab and said, "Zoom." He twisted his head. "Stanton?"

"Yes?"

"Can your boys do a spy sweep?"

"Yes, but why? Katie said Singh checked this room for bugs once a month."

"Humor me."

Stanton talked with one of the investigators, who then took a device out of a satchel and stood in the middle of the room while holding it in front of him as he pointed in all directions. After a moment the investigator knitted his brow and walked to a far wall. He leaned in to stare at a picture before taking a small knife out of his pocket and scraping something from the edge. The investigator held his hand out to Stanton. She used her index and thumb to take hold of the small object and examined it closely.

"What do you make of this?" Stanton walked over to Heart.

He looked at the small object and then back out the window. He again checked left and right.

"What are you looking at?"

"Remember at Imperial Towers when I saw a flivver at the opposite building? I thought I saw something. It occurred to me our killer was listening for our discovery of the body. Even watching."

He turned to look at the forensics team. "Everything under control here?"

"Looks to be," Stanton said.

"Who's next on the list?"

"Ashaki Okafor."

"Let's go."

***

"Okafor has a reputation for being a tough businesswoman — truly a cutthroat at the table." Stanton spoke in hushed tones, even though they were seated in the far corner of the reception area. "However, she is the leading philanthropist in the city. While she's amassed a fortune, she's recognized she can't take it with her, and she gives back more than any other person on the council."

"That would make me believe she wouldn't be the one wanting to take over power." Heart kept his eyes on the police officer at the reception desk.

"Good point."

"I wonder if she's making us wait for the sake of making us wait — a psychological ploy to get us off balance."

"Well..."

"Once a player, always a player."

A well-dressed man emerged from a door on the other side of reception. "If you will follow me, Ms. Okafor will see you now."

Heart and Stanton followed the man to a large double door. He held his right hand to a wall scanner and the twin doors slid apart. "Follow me." He led them across a room laid out as more of a living room in a home than an office. Another set of twin doors opened, and they walked out onto a terrace.

An elderly woman came forward. "Detective Heart. Sergeant Stanton." She smiled and held out her hand. "Ashaki Okafor. Call me Ashaki. Please, make yourselves comfortable." She gestured to a coffee table surrounded by easy chairs. "I've asked my satrap, my senior advisor, to be present. Charlie?" A man approached from the opposite side of the patio. "This is Charlie Vance."

Heart stiffened.

Vance grinned. "Hello, Matthew. Long time no see."

Okafor raised her brow. "You two know each other?"

"We've had a passing acquaintance." Vance stepped

forward and shook hands with Stanton. "Sergeant." He turned to the detective and stuck out his hand, but Heart had already sat down.

"Ms. Okafor," Heart said, "I mean, Ashaki. Sorry." Okafor smiled. "We're here to investigate—"

"The murder of Willard Bachmann."

"Ah, you're in the know."

"I have my sources. Although the chief assigning me protection leads me to believe my name may be on somebody's list."

"Singh is dead."

Okafor remained still, mulling over the news.

"Is Ashaki in danger?" Vance looked suspicious.

"We don't know, Mr. Vance." Heart glared at him. "We don't want to take any unnecessary risks."

"Detective Heart," Okafor said, "is it your supposition the OligCouncil itself is the target of a vendetta?"

"It seems to have been common knowledge a power play was going on. The death of Bachmann was interpreted as the first step of a new approach in dealing with politics."

Okafor chuckled. "Oh, come now. There has always been the back-and-forth with the various members trying to get to the top. However, everybody knew they were dependent on one another, and any one-upmanship was viewed in the friendly manner of a tennis game. Nobody gets hurt."

"Two out of five makes me think somebody wants someone to get hurt."

"Am I under suspicion?"

Heart looked at her soberly. "No offense, but we must consider all possibilities."

Okafor turned to Vance and smiled. "You told me, Charlie, that I had a killer instinct for business. I hadn't thought you were being literal."

"Ashaki," Vance said, "I'm advising you to take this matter seriously. I think Detective Heart has made a good point. Something is going on."

Okafor got up and started pacing. "All right. But what are

you proposing? I have protection. Does this mean I have to curtail my activities? Do I stop going out? This week alone I have at least five charity events, and on Saturday I'm supposed to cut the ribbon for a new arts museum on the East Side."

"I can handle everything."

"That's appreciated, Charlie, but bear in mind this is my life's work. I don't want to stop living."

Vance folded his arms. "I want to stop you from dying. There's a nut out there, and we can't take a chance of them getting to you. This won't last forever. I'm sure the detective and the sergeant will apprehend the culprit."

Okafor stopped pacing and looked at Heart. "Where are you in your investigation? Any leads?"

"We're looking into a number of things. All criminals make a mistake."

"True. Then again, how many will die before that mistake is made?"

"We'll do our best," Stanton said.

Okafor shot her a critical glance. "I hope that's good enough." She held out her hand, first to Heart and then to Stanton. "Good luck, officers. If there's anything else I can do, please contact my office. They know how to get ahold of me."

"Thank you, Ms. Okafor," Heart said. "I mean Ashaki."

"Charlie will show you out."

They watched Ashaki Okafor cross the terrace and go inside.

"Thank you for your inquiry, and thank you for your protection." Vance shook Stanton's hand. "I'm surprised to see you again, Heart."

"No thanks to you, Vance," Heart said. "I ought to bust you one right in the chops."

Vance took a step back and held up his hands. "Hey, I wasn't the one who meddled in other people's affairs. If you choose to play with the big boys, you must be ready to concede the game. Winner takes all. Loser shown no mercy."

"You cheated."

"Winning at all costs. No one remembers the losers."

"How do you sleep at night?"

"Quite nicely, thank you. The finest sheets, the best bed, a luxurious apartment. I'm comfortable in my misery."

Heart stepped toward Vance, grabbing him by the lapel of his jacket and forcing him to back into a low flower planter. He pushed Vance off balance and held him over the planter.

Vance smirked. "Temper, temper."

Heart smirked back and let go.

Vance fell backward, disappearing over the side of the flower box.

"Heart!" Stanton rushed forward and leaned over. Vance was sprawled on a ledge a meter below the terrace, swearing angrily.

Stanton turned to Heart. "Damn, I thought you dropped him off the building." She looked down on Vance. "How did you know the ledge was there?" Heart was stomping toward to the door and she rushed to follow. "You did know, right?"

They left the office and headed for the elevators.

"What was all that about?" she asked again.

"He's the guy who had me demoted to the settlements."

"Really?"

"Really." Heart scowled. "And as you can see, he couldn't care less what he does or who he does it to, as long as it serves his interests."

"You're pissed."

"No shit. How would you like it if your life was taken away from you?" Heart pursed his lips as he stared at her pointed expression. Hanging his head, he massaged a temple. "Listen, I'm sorry. That was inappropriate. I was way out of line." He shook his head. "God, I'm an idiot," he said, looking her in the eye. "I'm sorry."

"Let's forget it and move on. We need to focus on finding our killer, Detective Heart."

"Okay."

They got into the elevator.

"I'd like to hear that story," she said, breaking the awkward silence.

"Sure," Heart said. "My tale of going from floater to grounder."

Chapter 6

Heart lounged back in the armchair. If he leaned to the right, he could see down the entire length of the side corridor to the front of the limoshuttle. The window shades were drawn, the lighting subdued. It was quiet, with just the background hum of machinery, punctuated by a voice somewhere up front. A flight attendant emerged from the galley.

"May I get you anything, Mr. Heart?"

"Do you have tea?"

"We have everything. Regular? Herbal?"

"Regular."

"We have a nice black Ceylon." She smiled. "And I have sugar biscuits. Sweet is nice with tea."

"Thank you."

She turned to the man sitting next to Heart. "And you, Mr. Delaney?"

"I'll have a coffee. Black. And I'll try one of those biscuits, too. Thanks."

The woman retreated up the passage.

Delaney spoke, his voice subdued. "As I was saying, Matt, these trips to the settlements are routine. Nothing to talk about — FS45 should be the same. However, there have been times when the settlers have gotten out of hand. Grounders hate floaters. They have as much chance as anybody else, but they're undisciplined and lazy. Rather than do something to improve themselves, they gripe. Most of them expect handouts instead of working. They always look for more credits. They never look for more work."

Heart leaned on his left elbow, listening intently.

"I want you to stick close to Vance," Delaney said. "Always pay attention to the crowd. You never know when some crazy may decide to step forward. And don't assume crazy means pushover. The settlements are home to ex-police and ex-military, including boots-on-the-ground soldiers from the last war. You could still have a run-in with a lunatic as well trained as yourself. Don't get complacent. You could end up with somebody handing you your ass on a plate."

"Okay, Bill." Heart chuckled, sure his superior was exaggerating.

"Don't laugh. A few months back, one of my personnel was stabbed." He shook his head. "With a fork."

"What?"

"Seriously. The company offered the farmers a catered meal during the last labor negotiations. Vance was presenting management's final offer when a settler got up from his table and began shouting in protest. One of my men stepped forward to escort him out, and the guy picked up his fork and stabbed him in the chest. Fortunately, it didn't go deep, but after my man retaliated by knocking the protester to the ground, a melee erupted between the settlers and security. We had to rush Vance out of the building. Fourteen people were arrested, and two of my people required medical attention. So, please, pay close attention and be ready for anything."

There was a chime and a melodious voice announced, "Landing in five minutes."

"The security detail will escort Vance into Headquarters and then lock down the building. He has a two-hour meeting with local representation."

The limoshuttle shifted. The lights came up full. Several men walked out of a side cabin and made their way to the front.

"Let's go." Delaney stood.

"Yes, sir."

Heart followed, and they joined four other men.

"Maazim, you're with me." Delaney gestured to a hulky bodyguard. "The rest of you exit first and secure the walk to the building. It's full sunlight. Use shades. Chayim and Jason to the right. Matt and David to the left."

Heart touched his ear-tab and a visor slid across his face, masking his eyes.

"Door."

Heart followed the team outside. The sun was overhead; the light was indeed bright. He scanned the area. The limoshuttle had landed in front of a building inside a temporary fence surrounding the perimeter. There was a crowd of people on the other side, looking in at the new arrivals. Several police officers were spaced out along the barrier, their backs to the building. Vance came out, flanked by Delaney and Maazim. Somebody booed as the three men marched inside. Heart heard a noise beside him. He looked down at a rock someone had thrown and then surveyed the crowd. Somebody raised their fist and shook it. He followed the rest of the security detail into the building.

A settler shook hands with Vance. "Good afternoon, Mr. Vance. I'm Cesar Estrada. I trust you had a pleasant trip."

"Let's skip the pleasantries. I want to discuss the latest quota. Things are not going well, and I want to know why."

"Yes, sir. Shall we go upstairs to the meeting room? It's the most comfortable."

Delaney barked out orders. "Matt, here. David, side exit on left. Chayim, side exit on right. Jason, you have the back. Maazim, with me." He turned to Vance. "Are you ready, sir?" Vance, Delaney, Maazim, and Cesar disappeared upstairs as the other guards marched down the center hall.

Heart looked around the plain, functional building. This part inside the door served as a waiting room; there were several chairs and two side tables. He paced, examining the furniture and the walls and glancing through the windows. Outside, a voice yelled, "Floater, go home!" Something hit the front door. He stepped closer to the window and looked out at the crowd.

"They hate your guts."

Heart turned around to find a blonde woman at the mouth of the hall. "I beg your pardon?"

"They detest you."

He looked outside again.

"Right now, your man is upstairs telling the union leader the company will not pay more: the farmers must work more."

He frowned at the woman. "And that's unfair?"

"The starting pay on the 'float is twenty credits per hour.

The starting pay on the ground is two credits per hour. How can anybody get ahead? Work more? Don't make me laugh." She smirked at Heart. "How much do you make?"

"That's personal."

"I bet you make at least eighty thousand a year. Maybe a hundred. I make twenty. Could you live on twenty thousand credits?"

"Well..."

"Not on the 'float. But you can scrape by on the ground. With help from friends and family."

A voice came from the top of the stairs. "Christine?"

The woman stepped to the bottom of the stairs. "Yes, Cesar?"

"Would you bring up the latest production statistics?"

"Right away." She glanced at Heart before heading down the hall to an office. He looked back out the window, curiously staring at the people. At the sound of returning footsteps, he cocked his head and watched the woman as she ascended the stairs.

More yelling came from outside, and Heart squinted through the window. His ear-tab beeped. "Matt, come upstairs," Delaney said. "I want you to stay with Vance."

He hurried up the stairs as Delaney and Maazim came running down. "We've got trouble brewing outside," Delaney said. "Don't let Vance out of your sight."

Heart nodded and strode from the stairway to a sparse room with a table and four chairs, remaining to one side. Vance sat at one end, in front of a large tablet, while Cesar and Christine stood behind him.

"Mr. Vance, my workers are doing the best they can," Cesar said. He pointed to the display. "Production levels have remained steady over the past month."

"If I compare this with last year," Vance said as he ran his finger over the screen, "I can see production has dropped by fifteen percent."

"But sir, the new irrigation system has proven to be faulty."

"I had expected people to work harder."

"But sir, everyone was promised a raise this year."

"I can't be handing out raises to people who don't produce."

Christine stepped forward, hands on her hips. "These people are trying to get by on a subsistence level. They can't make ends meet. They barely have enough to eat. How can you expect them to work harder?"

Vance pushed back in his seat and regarded the woman. "And you are?"

"Elbe. Christine Elbe."

"Mx. Elbe, I'm not running a charity here."

Christine pursed her lips. "Mr. Vance, you come from privilege, while these people are living in poverty. Where's their motivation to work hard if they have no chance of getting ahead?"

He contemplated the woman's words as he adjusted a cuff of his shirt. Without taking his eyes away from Christine, he said, "Cesar, would you give us a moment?"

"Pardon?"

"I would like a word with Mx. Elbe in private."

Cesar stared at Vance.

"I want you to leave the room."

Cesar hesitated, confused. "Uh, okay." He walked toward the stairs, looked back, and then left the room.

Vance stood and put his hands behind his back. Pacing the length of the table, he paused and then walked back to Christine. He looked at her before he whipped up his right hand and slapped her across the cheek. The bare walls amplified the sound of the blow. Heart took a tentative step forward, shocked. Christine covered the side of her face, staring wide-eyed at Vance.

"Mx. Elbe, I'm in charge here. Don't you ever speak to me like that again." Vance loomed over the woman. "You're a lazy lot. You expect to be rewarded for doing little or nothing. That's not how to get ahead in the world."

"You bastard," Christine hissed.

Vance raised his hand and scowled. "You impudent little—

"

Heart seized Vance's wrist. "Mr. Vance!"

Vance attempted to tug his arm free, but Heart held fast. The two men glared at each other.

"Let go," Vance said.

"Yes, sir."

Vance sat back down and pointed at Christine. "Send Cesar back up and get out."

She gritted her teeth as she caressed her cheek. She shot a glance at Heart before returning to stare at the back of Vance's head.

"Now, Mx. Elbe." Vance tapped a finger on the table.

Christine huffed and then stomped across the room and marched downstairs. After a moment, Cesar returned.

"This is my final word," Vance said. "I expect the new irrigation system to be up and running by the end of the month. If it's not, your head is on the block. There will be no raise. Your people have failed to meet quotas, and their overall production is down from last year. They should all feel lucky I do not cut their pay. I give them a salary for their work. I expect something in return. If they do not give me what I want, I will stop giving them what they want. Warn them. I'm putting all of you on notice, as I will not tolerate an unprofitable enterprise. If there's no profit, there's no point in doing this."

He got up. "Make this happen for me, and there will be something in it for you. Don't disappoint me."

"Yes, sir." Cesar stood deferentially out of the way as Vance headed for the stairway.

Heart followed and touched his ear-tab. "Matt here. We're ready to leave."

There was a beep and Delaney said, "Exit and proceed straight to the limoshuttle."

Vance got to the front door and grabbed the handle. He stopped and turned. "What's your name?"

"Matthew Heart, sir."

Vance eyed him. "Heart, your job is security. My job is

business. I don't interfere with your job. You don't interfere with mine."

Their eyes remained locked on one another in silent battle.

"Yes, sir."

Vance opened the door and stepped outside, Heart following close. They met an angry mob. There were now three times as many people pushing against the fence, shaking their fists, and yelling. Someone had thrown several bottles of paint against the vehicle, and colorful splotches marred its slick black exterior. At the sight of Vance, the crowd became more vocal.

Delaney waved at Heart. "Hurry. I've got reinforcements, but they won't last long. We need to get out of here right now."

Heart and Vance jogged across the gap to the limoshuttle. Delaney ushered them through the entry before stepping in himself. As the door automatically shut, he yelled, "Go!" The vehicle jerked as it lifted. Some object bounced off the exterior with a clang.

Each agent called for their eye shields as mist hissed from nozzles surrounding them and a bright light scanned from floor to ceiling. The inner door of the decontamination vestibule opened, and everyone exited. Heart moved to a window, looking out at the ground below. Hundreds of people were milling about. The news of Vance's arrival had spread throughout the settlement.

"That was close," Delaney said.

"What happened?" Heart asked.

"I don't know, but the settlers were none too pleased about our presence. A few people swelled to hundreds and, as you saw, they were growing hostile. I called the local police for support, but it was inevitable a few cops could not hold back a mob of angry people."

"Do the grounders hate us that much?"

"People can be envious, and envy can turn to hate."

At this, Heart made his way down the passage and took his original armchair. The lounge area was empty. He touched his ear-tab, and the integrated screen curved around his eyes. "Search. Vance, Charles." He read several newspaper articles, some opinion pieces. However, he found there was little about the man himself, and any information about his business was general. "Search. Settlements, average wages." More information, but again short on specifics. A government source mentioned a minimum wage of five credits an hour while emphasizing this was a guideline, not a rule.

Delaney came out of a cabin ahead and gestured to Heart.

Heart got up and walked to the front. "Yes?"

"Mr. Vance wants to see you." He pressed his thumb to a reader and the door slid open. He waved Heart in.

Heart stepped inside and Delaney followed, the door closing behind him. Vance stared at a display. "Heart? It is Heart, isn't it?"

"Yes, sir."

"I cannot tolerate disobedience."

Heart furrowed his brow.

Delaney turned toward him and leaned close, whispering, "Sorry, kid." Then he wound up and punched him in the stomach. Heart doubled over, gasping.

"I cannot tolerate disloyalty," Vance said.

Delaney bent slightly and slammed a fist into Heart's cheek, dropping him to the floor. Heart lay on his side, his head ringing. He was shocked and disoriented.

"I'll no longer be requiring your services, Mr. Heart." Vance turned and looked at the man on the floor. "Get him out of here. Dump him."

Delaney touched a wall control, and the door slid open. Two other guards came in, each picking Heart up by one arm. They forced him out of the cabin and led him to the front of the limoshuttle. The outer door slid open, showing they had landed. The two men pushed him and he tripped, falling face-first onto the earth and tasting dust. The heat of the mid-afternoon sun bore down on the back of his neck. There was a noise from behind, and he twisted around to see the limoshuttle rise and move off.

Heart rose unsteadily and looked around. As far as he could see in any direction, there were swaths of plowed, dry land, broken up by irrigation ditches and dirt laneways. He touched his ear-tab to activate the display. "Connect." He studied the readout. "System Check." There was no signal available. "Sunglasses." His visor slid across his face as he held one hand to his brow and scanned the horizon. Way off in the distance, what looked to be a communications tower wavered in the heat. He sighed and headed up a dirt track. It was too difficult to estimate the distance, and he prepared himself for a long walk. He gingerly touched his cheek and wondered if he'd end up with a black eye.

After trudging through the heat for what seemed like an eternity, Heart stopped and raised a hand to shield his eyes. There were structures in the distance, but he still couldn't judge how far away they were. Taking off his suit jacket, he hung the collar over his head, letting the rest of it drape down his back. The sky was blue — not a cloud in sight. With the sun beating down, beads of sweat formed in various spots under his clothes.

He marched on. Parched, he looked around in the hope of finding a source of water. The scorching heat enveloped him, and he had long given up the idea of staying dry. His shirt was soaked, his underwear wet. Beads of moisture slid down his thighs. The thought of a cold drink spurred him on toward the now-visible buildings of a settlement.

At a crossroad stood a sign, with an arrow pointing toward the structures, that read Farm Settlement 45. Vance had landed at least ten kilometers outside of town just to make Heart walk for hours, ensuring he would be back at the metrofloat by the time Heart reached civilization. Was that part of the plan? There could be little doubt Vance knew what he was doing. Delaney and the others acted as if they had done this before. Was this punishment because Heart had pissed him off? Or had it been planned? But that didn't make sense because Heart had just met the man. "Connect." There was still no signal available.

Heart plodded on, finally arriving at an isolated block structure. There was a single door facing the track. Beside it, a pipe stuck out of the ground, ending in a faucet. He turned the tap and water poured out, pooling in the dirt below. Happily, he felt the water and then cupped his hands and scooped some up to his mouth. After tasting it, he put his mouth to the stream and sucked in several refreshing mouthfuls.

Heart tapped his ear-tab to retract his sunglasses and splashed water on his face. He stood back up, wiping the sleeve of his shirt over his forehead and cheeks as he turned off the faucet.

"You're not a farmer."

A panting dog was sniffing his pant leg. Its hindquarters rested on a two-wheel cart as it had no back legs, and one front leg was amputated at the elbow, replaced by a metal tube. Heart touched his ear-tab for the visor and looked around.

"Are you a floater?"

Heart peered around the corner of the structure. A little girl with a prosth leg eyed him.

He nodded. "Oh, hello. Do you live around here?"

Without taking her eyes off him, she pointed in the general direction of the buildings.

"I need to get home," he said.

"Are you a floater?"

"Yes."

"Did you fall off?"

He smirked. "No, I didn't." He leaned against the wall. "I need help."

"Mom goes to Wang."

"Who's Wang?"

"He makes food."

"You mean a restaurant?"

"No. A counter. With stools."

"Where do I find him?"

He looked in the direction she pointed and saw an open space between cement-block dwellings. "Up there?"

"Yes. Go straight."

Heart studied the girl. "What's your name?"

"Sally. What's yours?"

"Matthew Heart."

"I don't think you can get home."

"Why not?"

"People come, but they never leave."

He ran a hand over his head, wiping it on the seat of his pants. "I've got to try. I hope this Wang can help me out." He looked toward the dwellings. "Can you show me the way?"

"Sure, it's not hard." Sally walked away.

"What about your dog?"

"He's not mine. He's a stray."

Heart followed. "So, you live with your mom?"

"Yes, the two of us."

Heart slowed down to match pace with Sally. "Why aren't you in school?"

"We got the afternoon off for the protest."

"Protest?"

"The floater came, and everybody wanted to go see him."

"Floater?"

"The boss. The man who runs the farms. He's not a nice person. Mom calls him a shit."

He glanced at her with a slight smile.

"This is where I live."

They walked by a two-story building: a wall of concrete bricks punctuated by windows, all with their blinds drawn. At the far end was a sign that read Low Cost Lodge.

"I have my own bedroom. It's one of the bigger apartments."

"What's your mother do?"

"She works for the farmers' union."

They approached the main entrance, which was surrounded by large windows. A front counter and a small waiting area were visible from the street. A man came out the door, walking with a mechanical tubular leg. One side of his head was made of a metallic skull and included an arti-eye. "Sally?"

"Hi, Mom." Sally hugged the man, and he leaned over to

kiss her forehead.

Sally turned back to Heart. "This is Matty."

Heart looked at the man. His face was partially done up with makeup: eyeshadow and lipstick.

"So, you've been dumped," the man said.

"Pardon?" Heart said.

The man held out his hand. "I'm Christine, Sally's mother. We met this morning at the farmers' union."

"Oh, yes." Heart hesitated and then shook his hand.

"Oh, Sally!" Christine said. "Poor Matty catches me all undone."

"Stop it, Mom. You always look good," Sally said.

Christine put an arm around Sally's shoulders and squeezed. "Aren't you the angel?" Christine grinned at Heart. "How can you not be charmed? It makes a girl feel good."

Heart smiled back. "Sally was telling me about somebody named Wang. I need help, and she suggested this Wang could do something. Would you be able to give me directions?"

"No problem." Christine pointed down the street. "Follow this lane down three corners and at the third, turn left. It's right there. He runs the local luncheon counter, although he's open all day. You can't miss the sign."

"Much obliged."

Heart started off, glancing back, curious.

Christine and Sally stood at the entrance, watching his retreat. "Why don't you help me select a wig for my date tonight? I am going to wear my pastel lavender dress, but I can't decide between black or red hair." She pulled open the door.

"Aw, come on, Mom. The boys like redheads."

They disappeared inside.

Heart counted down the streets and turned left onto a boulevard that split the settlement in two. Various shops lined each side. People were milling about, and some children played with a ball in the middle of the street. One door down stood a luncheon counter with a line of stools facing the street. Several men sat eating, while a wrinkled man with prosthetic arms and legs moved between grill and refrigerator. Matt watched as he picked up a frying pan and used a fork to scoop something onto a plate before placing the dish in front of a customer.

Heart sat down on a stool at the far end and took a menu held between a container of utensils and a napkin dispenser.

The man behind the counter came over. "What can I get you?"

"How about a cup of coffee?" Heart ran a finger down the list of items. "The All-Day Breakfast." He looked up. "And help." He stuck out his hand. "Matthew Heart."

The man looked at Heart and then at the offered hand. After a moment, he wiped his palm on his apron and shook it. "Wang. Just Wang. Coffee and breakfast are easy. Help may not be."

"I need to get back to Metrofloat New York."

"Good luck."

"That's it?"

Wang snorted. "It's not like there's a regular shuttle going back and forth. Supply trucks, yes. But passengers? Going to the settlements is mostly a one-way street. Once somebody comes, they rarely leave." He wandered down the counter and picked up a pot of coffee and a mug, setting the cup down in front of Heart. "The policy of all floats is to avoid ground contamination, right?" He poured the coffee. "Nobody wants to see necrofasc introduced into urban areas. Even though medical science has got a handle on the problem, and transmission only occurs under particular circumstances, there is a lot of fear and prejudice about the disease." He set the pot down and crossed his arms. "Who are you, and how did you get here?"

"I came with the limoshuttle today."

"You were with Vance?"

"Yes."

Wang laughed. "You are so screwed."

"What do you mean?"

"You're not the first. When Vance gets pissed off with somebody, he dumps them out here. But that isn't enough. He gets them banned from the metrofloat. Even if they find transportation back to the city, they no longer have security clearance and can't get in. Vance is such a prick. I thought he was terrible to the settlers, but he's got a mean streak in him and he'll screw you up the ass if he thinks you looked at him the wrong way."

Wide-eyed, Heart looked at Wang but said nothing.

Wang laughed again. "Let me get your breakfast," he said, wandering back to the grill.

Heart touched his ear-tab. "Connect." It was odd there was no connection, no signal at all. "System Check." The device seemed to be operating normally, and there should be a signal in the settlement. Had Vance cut him off from the system? Had he remotely disabled Heart's device? "Security." He sipped his coffee as he examined the various parameters. "Verify." After a moment, a message appeared: Access denied. He frowned. "Verify identity Bravo Alfa four-two-seven-seven." After another moment, he saw the chilling words: "BA4277 does not exist."

Wang had walked back down the length of the counter and set a plate in front of Heart. "I assume, from the look on your face, things don't bode well."

"I'm not just persona non grata. I don't seem to exist."

Wang nodded. "I've seen this before. An identity is temporarily disabled, effectively wiping that person from the system. As I said, even if you find transport you'll never be allowed to land."

"What am I going to do?"

"You can go to the local precinct. You'll spend hours and hours as those bumblers try to do something. However, they'll only be partially successful. Vance is at the top, and whatever he does cascades down the ranks. The chance of you finding somebody at the bottom able to affect those at the top is slim."

Heart ran one hand through his hair in frustration. "Aw, shit!"

"Aw shit, indeed. You'll get yourself reinstated, but you'll struggle to regain your security clearance. The only way is to find somebody at the same level as Vance, but since you can't even go to Metrofloat New York, you'll never get the opportunity to find anybody, never mind talk to them. Maybe, just maybe, you could find someone with connections, but there's not much chance of that at this settlement. We're the poor unknowns. We don't matter to anyone. Nobody cares about us. Nobody knows we even exist."

Heart stared off into space, tapping his fingers on the counter.

Wang put both of his mechanical hands on the counter and leaned over. "Hey!"

Heart shook himself from his brooding. "What?"

"Eat your food before it gets cold." Wang straightened. "And don't forget to enjoy it. It's on the house."

"Why would you do that?"

"You don't have an identity. No ID, no profile. No profile means no finances. No finances, no credits. How do you expect to pay?" Wang strolled down the counter and started speaking to another customer.

Heart stared at his plate, still drumming his fingers in reflection. Finally, he took a fork from among the utensils and ate the food while sipping his coffee.

Wang came back with the pot and refilled his mug. He pulled out a hand-tab from under the counter. "What's your ID?"

"Bravo Alfa four-two-seven-seven."

Wang tapped a finger on the device and studied the display. "As far as I can tell, you are active on the metrofloat. However, your ID has been rendered inactive here at FS45. I'm guessing the local system will resync with Central and you'll come back online, but for the moment you remain an unknown. You don't exist."

"Really?"

"By rendering your ID inactive, Vance disconnected you from local communications."

"It was a long walk."

"You can stay the night here. I've got a room out back."

"I couldn't."

Wang chuckled. "You couldn't? Buddy, you don't seem to have grasped your predicament. You have no credits. You can't pay for this meal, never mind paying for accommodation. Without an ID, you can't phone home to mommy and daddy. Nobody is coming to your rescue. You're out in the middle of nowhere with only the shirt on your back. You're screwed, and you're screwed royally. If you don't accept my kind and generous offer, you're going to be sleeping on the streets tonight."

"Why are you doing this?"

"Like all the grounders around here, I have no love for the floaters. But Vance? He's a nasty piece of work. He does everything in his power to make the situation between the settlements and the metrofloat that much worse. Everybody wants a fair shake and to find their place in the sun. He's got privilege, entitlement, and prejudice up the ass, and he's not going to let anybody else forget it."

"Hi, Wang."

He looked up and smiled. "Hey."

Heart turned around to find Christine and Sally walking toward them.

Wang maneuvered around the end of the counter, hugging Sally and kissing Christine on the cheek. "How are you doing? You look terrific tonight."

"Stop it, Wang. You're going to make me blush."

Heart inspected Christine, finding her ensemble — dress, shoes, makeup, and hair — attractive.

Wang said, "Have you met Heart? He'll be staying with us for a while."

"Yes, we have," Christine said, brushing aside her red hair.

"Hi, Matty," Sally said.

"Hi, Sally."

"Good evening." Christine nodded to Heart.

Heart tipped his head in a silent greeting.

"So, Sally," Wang said, "are you going to help me with dinner tonight? I expect the afternoon shift will come by and it'll be busy."

"I'll load the dishwasher."

Wang grinned. "Good girl."

"I'll be back by nine," Christine said. "I told my date I can only stay for dinner."

"We'll be here. Have fun."

Christine turned. "Nice to see you again, Matty," she said before starting up the street.

Heart rotated on his stool and watched her go.

"Mommy's pretty." Sally stood, looking at Heart.

He nodded. "Yes, she is."

Wang leaned over the counter. "Hey, time's a wastin'. I need my kitchen helper."

Sally grinned as she ran around the end of the counter. "Yes, Chief."

"Heart?" Wang said.

"Yes?"

"I want you to go to the local precinct and talk with Sergeant Hooper. He'll see about syncing Local with Central to reactivate your ID. He can confirm your status, but I suspect your security clearance for the metrofloat has been revoked. Unless you've got friends in high places, you're not getting back in. I'm sure you're going to need time to digest this, but you better get used to the idea that the settlement is your new home." Wang followed after Sally and said over his shoulder, "Welcome to the ground."

Chapter 7

Heart crossed his legs and stared at Stanton, relieved at having told his story.

"I would have dropped him off the building, too," she said.

"City Ordinance Five Twenty-One states any outdoor area not surrounded by a barrier of at least one point five meters must have a security ledge no farther than one meter down from said area."

"Clever."

"Who's next on the list?"

"Keith Rupert. Ninety-four years old. Resides at the Grace Abbey Nursing Home."

"Nursing home?"

"Yes. His health is failing, but he's lucid."

"How does he participate on the OligCouncil?" Heart asked.

"Remotely. I don't think he's attended in person for years. While power does mean presence, he makes his power felt by proxy, and he's involved in the day-to-day operations of his businesses and the council. It's a family enterprise, and his two daughters run the place. They do their dad proud. The Rupert name is everywhere — stamped on all aspects of life on the metrofloat. No one can say for sure, but when Keith passes, one daughter is expected to take over on the council."

"If Rupert is out of it, could a daughter be our killer?"

"Anything is possible. Let's check it out."

The flivver pulled out into traffic and negotiated its way into the major flyway for crosstown access.

"May I ask you a personal question?" Stanton kept her eyes on the traffic.

"Shoot."

"What happened to your parents?"

"They were killed in a traffic accident fifteen years ago. My dad was a cop. I'm happy they got to see their son follow in his footsteps, but I'm not sure they would have been happy I left the force to go into private security. They definitely wouldn't have been happy about me ending up in the settlements." He glanced out the window. "At least I can say life has never been dull."

The autopilot took them out of the corridor, and the flivver dropped to street level. It then drove up half a block, pulling into a medical facility. Stanton and Heart left the vehicle, which disappeared into the autopark. They made their way to a luxury suite on the eighth floor, where a police officer nodded to them as they walked through the door. An old man was propped up in bed. His eyes were shut, and he looked to be asleep. The wall over his head held a large display showing various medical readouts. Heart noticed a line graph with intermittent spikes showing cardiac activity.

A nurse sitting to one side got up and came over, whispering, "May I help you?"

"We're with MetPol," Stanton said.

"Ah yes, Chief Voynich said you would come over."

"Can we talk to Mr. Rupert?"

The three of them looked at the elderly council member.

"He's been napping for a while. Let me rouse him. It's time for his medication, anyways."

The nurse walked over to the bed and touched the man's shoulder. "Mr. Rupert?"

His eyes opened.

"You have visitors. And it's time for your medication."

"Who's here?"

"There are two people from the police." The nurse waved them over.

The man hadn't moved, but his eyes followed first one, then the other, as Heart and Stanton came to stand on either side of the bed.

"Mr. Rupert? I'm Sergeant Stanton, and this is Detective Heart. We're with the MetPol. We'd like to ask you a few questions."

He stared at Stanton, moving his mouth, though they could hear no words.

"Pardon?" Stanton leaned closer.

"How many are dead so far?"

Stanton and Heart looked at one another.

"Sir?" Stanton said.

"How many of the council have been killed so far?"

"You know about this?"

"How many?"

"Two. Bachmann and Singh."

Rupert became agitated. "I'm next."

Heart glanced at the wall display and noticed the heart rate had increased. "How do you know that, Mr. Rupert?"

"Isn't it obvious? He wants to take over and be dictator. He wants to dispense with us, the little people, and control everything."

"Who, Mr. Rupert?"

"I told him he was mad. That's not the way the world works. We bring order to the chaos. We bring stability and peace. Who wants to return to anarchy?"

"Who are you talking about, Mr. Rupert?"

"Bachmann was a fool."

"Willard Bachmann?"

"That thing is crazy."

"But Bachmann is dead."

"It'll be the death of us all."

A warning buzzer sounded and Heart looked up to see a red light flashing.

The nurse jumped up. "Stand back." She touched her ear-tab. "Code Blue! Code Blue!"

Heart looked back at Rupert and saw the man was still. He wasn't breathing.

A woman and a man in medical uniforms burst into the room. The man pointed at Stanton and Heart. "Out!"

They backed up, watching the staff move around Rupert. Heart took Stanton's arm and led her back out the door.

"So, what did that mean?" he asked.

"Earlier, I said he was lucid. Maybe I was wrong."

"Bachmann is dead, right?"

"We matched his ID chip from the left arm. We verified

fingerprints and DNA. It all matched. The body we picked up at FS45 was Willard Bachmann. There is no doubt about it."

Heart gazed down the hall. "Is Rupert delusional, or did he give us a clue?"

"What? You're saying Bachmann has come back from the dead to haunt us?"

"Okay, that sounds absurd. But is something else going on? Something we've yet to discover?"

"Like what?"

"We've been thinking about the council itself, and its members. What if we expanded our investigation to others, those second in command? Vance is a prick — he's always been a prick — but he's also always been a prince, never a king. Have his ambitions grown over the years? He's aligned himself with Ashaki Okafor, but is that a mere stepping stone to his real goal of gaining more power? Should Okafor be watching her back? Although I find it hard to believe Vance would bump off the entire council to seize control of the city. That's too ambitious, even for him."

The female medic came out of Mr. Rupert's room. "We have him stabilized on life support. However, I'm afraid he won't be able to talk anymore. At least, not for the moment."

"We understand," Stanton said.

"Just to let you know, Mr. Rupert has given specific instructions for no heroic measures to be taken. He's signed a health care directive saying he does not want to be kept alive and prefers to let nature take its course. He's had his time, and he's ready to move on."

"Thank you."

"I would advise you to check back in tomorrow. I'm assuming this crisis will have calmed down by then, and Mr. Rupert will be able to see visitors again. Call first, though. Whoever is on duty can give you the latest update. He naps throughout the day, so if you do visit, it's best to time it for when he's awake."

"Thanks."

The two officers walked to the elevators and rode down to

the ground floor, both lost in thought.

"It's seventeen hundred," Stanton said. "Let's check in with Voynich."

They returned to their flivver and Heart put the communicator on the console. He touched Call and put the device on speaker. After giving a brief update, he described their plans for the evening, which involved seeing the final council member. Heart mentioned Vance and their idea somebody other than the council members could be complicit in the murders.

"After our visit with Chaska Enapay this evening, we may have a better idea of where to go from there," he said.

"Just a moment," Voynich said. There were muffled voices in the background. "I've just been told Keith Rupert died ten minutes ago."

Heart and Stanton glanced at each other, shocked.

"The daughters are being called in. The presiding doctor will sign the death certificate, and the body will be released later this evening. Nobody is questioning natural causes, and there is no suggestion of foul play. An autopsy will not be performed."

"I have a suggestion," Heart said.

"Let's hear it."

"Can you get authorization for a memory reconstruction?"

"Why?"

"Rupert said some odd things during our interview, which leads me to believe he knew more about Bachmann than we understood. We shouldn't pass up the opportunity to delve further into his relationship with Bachmann."

"I don't know if the daughters would protest or not. I'd have to get a court order, and it's after seventeen hundred. That might not be so easy at this hour." Voynich sneezed. "Sorry. Let me look into this and get back to you. In the meantime, carry on with your evening and keep me apprised of your findings. Voynich out."

***

They arrived at Enapay's office at nineteen hundred hours. As with the visit with Rupert, police officers stood at the door.

"Good luck seeing him," one of the officers said.

"Why? What's wrong?" Stanton said.

"He got scared and hired several bodyguards this afternoon. Has them stationed all around him — and I mean all around him. He refuses to come out and even sent a guard out for food."

Stanton touched the door display. "Mr. Enapay?"

The display lit up and a close-up of a face appeared, as if it were peering out. "Are you the police Chief Voynich sent over?"

"Yes, sir."

The door slid open, revealing a hulk in a tight-fitting suit. He scrutinized them before moving aside and gesturing that they could enter. Heart glanced at the guard as they walked by.

Enapay sat on a couch behind a low table, a hand-tab in front of him. Two guards leaned on the back of the sofa at either end.

"Pull up a chair," Enapay said, pointing to two straight-back chairs on the opposite side of the table.

Taking a seat, Stanton introduced herself and Heart. "We'd like to ask you a few questions."

"Ask away. I have nothing to hide. In fact, I have everything to gain if I can help in any way to get this crazed lunatic behind bars."

"What do you know?"

"Bachmann's dead. Singh's dead. Rupert died today, but I'm certain that will turn out to be murder, too. It's down to dear old Okafor and myself. Since I'm innocent, you must conclude that bitch Okafor is not above killing the competition. I never liked that woman. I suspect she is capable of evil things. She may be a philanthropist now, but she didn't get all that money by being nice. No sirree, she'd just as soon cut your throat as smile at you."

There was a crash from behind. Enapay jumped up and put

a foot on the seat of the couch, scrambling over the back and disappearing from sight. Stanton and Heart whipped around to see the burly guard sitting on the edge of the office desk, looking down. On the floor were pieces of an ornate glass lamp. He stooped down, picking up the pieces with one hand and placing them in his other. "Sorry, Mr. Enapay. I didn't see it."

Enapay peeked over the back of the sofa. Stanton, Heart, and the other two guards looked at the spooked councilor. He stood, pulling on his lapels to straighten his jacket. "You can't be too careful," he said, walking around the end of the couch and sitting back down.

"Has this ever happened before?" Stanton asked.

"Yes, I think the cleaning staff broke a decorative vase last year."

"No, sir. I mean the council. Has there ever been an incident so confrontational that one member would want to hurt another?"

"No. I thought we all got along well, considering that in some areas we're business competitors."

"Ashaki Okafor said a similar thing."

"Okafor is a nice lady," Enapay said. "I've always liked her."

Stanton's gaze flitted to Heart, and he shrugged at the contradiction. "Has anybody ever talked about taking over?" she asked.

Enapay frowned. "Taking over?"

"Taking over the OligCouncil."

"I'm not sure I know what you mean. We switch places every year, taking turns being the head of the council. It's all democratic and is in the best interests of everybody. It's not like any one of us gets an unfair advantage over the others. Okay, there are minor skirmishes from time to time, but these are easily solved within our group. Nobody gains anything by declaring war on anybody else. There's too much at stake. There's too much to lose. Why rock the boat when there's so much to be gained by working together?"

"You paint a rosy picture, Mr. Enapay. But here you sit, scared. What do you think is going on?"

"I haven't got a clue," Enapay said, clearly agitated.

"Do you think a member of the council is trying to take over?"

"As I said, everyone gets their turn as the head of the council."

"Do you think somebody's trying to destroy the council?"

"Destroy it? Why would somebody do that?"

"To become the single power. To become a dictator."

Enapay rubbed his hands together, fiddling with his nails. "I don't see how such a thing would be possible. A dictator requires military force to seize control, but our system involves free enterprise. Dictatorships seek to suppress such freedoms for the sake of control. Free enterprise leads to profit! I would argue a dictatorship is not profitable. Certainly not over the long run. Why do something if it's not profitable? What's the point? Nobody's going to do something if there isn't a benefit, a reward, for doing so."

Heart leaned forward and stared into the councilor's bloodshot eyes. "Mr. Enapay, could there be somebody else? Somebody in the wings who may have something to gain if the council disappeared?"

"Are you familiar with history, Detective Heart?"

"The wars? Why don't you tell me your version?"

"The ravages of disease decimated the planet. Mankind almost wound up as extinct as the dinosaurs. Those who remained had to deal with anarchy. We reverted to the tried-and-true method of social order: might is right. The strong do what they can, and the weak suffer what they must. However, the discovery of antigravity literally lifted us out of the dirt. We rose to the skies and developed a new order, guided by mutual interest. It wasn't perfect but it was orderly. And profitable."

"And do you think that profit model was equitable for everyone?"

"No system is perfect. Not everyone can sit at the top. There are leaders and there are followers. There are more followers than leaders, but there is order. The opposite of order is chaos, and that isn't good for anybody. It is better to have order and profit, even a small profit, than chaos and no profit. Or death."

Heart sat back up, slinging one arm over the back of the chair. He studied Enapay. "Have you ever visited the ground?"

"No."

"Never?"

"I never wanted to take that chance."

"Why not?"

"I'm whole. I have every intention of staying that way."

"A lot of people don't have that choice."

"I said no system was perfect. However, it's better than the alternative."

"Let's come back to the council. What could be gained from the death of its members?"

Enapay looked off and scratched his chin. "Well, each member is the head of an organization. Within each organization there is a structure. In that sense, the hierarchy would handle the loss of the head. There is succession planning. Business continuity also deals with leadership issues, and there are plans for vacations, sickness, and even death. Life will not stop."

"Getting rid of the head of each of the five organizations would introduce a measure of instability in your order."

"Yes, I suppose, but life would go on. Don't forget, everyone has a personal stake in keeping the order. No one wants to risk having the lights go out."

"You're talking about the big picture. What about the little picture?"

"What do you mean?" Enapay asked.

"Metrofloat New York has crime: people steal, people vandalize, people do terrible things. What happens to their personal stake? I would think not everybody sees things in such terms as you. In those cases, it's them against the city, them against the system. For example, I'm a little guy trying to get what I can. I don't see the big picture at all."

"You've lost me."

Heart swept one arm across the room. "You have position. You have power. You've got stuff. You want to keep order because you want to protect your life, but what about the guy who has less? In fact, he has so little he's willing to do anything to get more. Heck, he may have nothing. Desperate times require desperate measures and all that. He may put order and stability at risk because that's his way of righting what he perceives as a wrong."

"What are you saying?"

"We started this investigation with the idea that one of the members of the OligCouncil wanted to take over. The more I think about it, the more I believe the threat is from the outside. Somebody wants to upset the balance to change something. Somebody is dissatisfied with the status quo."

There was a moment of silence. Everyone looked askance, avoiding each other's gaze.

"Mr. Enapay," Heart said, "do you know the minimum wage for farmers?"

"Uh, hmm. I believe it's five credits an hour. No, wait. The council raised it to six credits two years ago."

"Your average farmer in FS45 is getting two credits an hour, sometimes one."

"How's that possible?"

"Greed, Mr. Enapay. People don't think they have enough and are willing to do anything to get more. Even if it means stepping on the little people."

"How do you know this?"

"I live in Farm Settlement Forty-Five."

Enapay looked him over. "You seem to be whole."

"I am. Good genes."

"Why are you investigating this case?"

"Chief Voynich and I go back a long way. I was born and raised here, and I know the city. But as an outsider, I bring an objective view." With that, Heart stood. "Mr. Enapay, we won't take up any more of your time."

Stanton now rose as well, and Heart held out his hand.

Enapay remained seated. "I'd rather not. No offense."

"None taken, but I'm not contagious."

"I got this far by being prudent, Detective Heart. Don't mind me if I don't change."

The husky guard escorted them to the door and thumbed a wall-tab. Heart and Stanton stepped into the hall and nodded a goodbye to the police officer.

"What do you make of him?" Stanton said as they walked back to their car.

"He knows no more than anybody else. Which is nothing."

Stanton stopped. "Just a sec. I have a message." She looked away, staring into the distance as she concentrated on the dispatch. "We have to go back to Grace Abbey."

"Why?"

"We've been asked to look at something — something that's not there."

"How's that possible?"

"Keith Rupert's brain is missing."

***

When Heart and Stanton arrived, a forensics crew was combing the room. The body of the deceased lay in his bed, propped up as they had first seen him. However, there was now a hole in the middle of his forehead. The team leader pointed to it, saying, "I've seen nothing like it. The entire brain has been removed from the skull. It's like it was sucked out of the cranium."

"Is there a device able to do that?" Heart leaned over, taking a closer look.

"Not that I know of. I can't think of any reason somebody would want to do this. If you wanted to study the brain, you'd study it intact. This would turn it into a jellified mass, so there wouldn't be much to study. It would be mush."

Stanton and Heart retreated to the hall to discuss the new development.

"I think we can see where this one is going," Heart said.

"Enapay has good reason to hide behind his couch." He pulled out the communicator. "Let's report this to Voynich. I'd say he'll want to beef up security for the last two members of the council, although I suspect the perpetrator is far more resourceful than we realize. I'm not sure a few more cops will stop him. Or her."

"Shall we go back to Headquarters?"

"Sure. Let's do some research. Rupert's raving about Bachmann got me thinking there may be more to Willard than meets the eye."

"He's dead."

"Yes. It's a great cover."

***

Stanton and Heart sat in a simple office, a wall display behind them. They had spent the past two hours poring over the files for all five members of the OligCouncil.

"I see nothing out of the ordinary," she said.

"Neither do I, but what Rupert said about Bachmann was confusing."

"What do you mean?"

"He first said Bachmann was a fool. *Was* a fool, not *is* a fool. Then he said, 'That thing is crazy.' He used the word *thing*. What was he referring to?"

"I have the recording."

"Call it up."

Stanton touched her hand-tab, and a video appeared on the display, showing the room from her angle as she'd stood over Rupert's bed. Only Mr. Rupert was visible, with Stanton speaking off-camera.

"I told him he was mad," Rupert said. "That's not the way the world works. We bring order to the chaos. We bring stability and peace. Who wants to return to anarchy?"

"Who are you talking about, Mr. Rupert?"

"Bachmann was a fool."

"Willard Bachmann?"

"That thing is crazy."

"But Bachmann is dead."

"It'll be the death of us all."

Stanton stopped the video. "You're right. He said 'thing.' Then he said, 'It'll be the death of us all.' It. Not he or she, but *it.*"

"We're looking for a man or a woman right now. Should we instead be looking for a machine?"

"Bachmann owned SynthResearch, the company that provided my new body. They're one of the largest providers of synthetic body parts."

"Don't they also do work in AI?"

"Everybody does. But, as far as I know, their main business is prosths."

"We should pay a visit tomorrow. Can you set it up?" Heart glanced at his hand-tab for the time. "It's been a long day. Let's call it a night."

"No point in going home. We start first thing in the morning. Let me get you a room. MetPol has an arrangement with the hotel across the street."

"That would be nice. Thanks," Heart said. "I'm feeling hungry and wouldn't mind a bite, with something to wash it down."

"I can suggest a place."

"You won't join me?"

"I don't go to bars."

He smiled. "Choose a place you like. I'm not inclined to drink alone."

***

They took a table tucked away in a corner, above the central dance floor. A few couples were gracefully moving through a cha-cha.

Heart picked up a menu-tab and studied the offerings. Glancing over the top edge, he noticed Stanton's eyes darting around. "Expecting someone?"

"No." She picked up her own menu-tab. "I haven't been in here in a while. It used to be popular with other members of the force."

"I think I'll have an arti-beer. No, wait. I'll have a white arti-wine with the beetle and worm stir-fry. That ought to satisfy my hunger and quench my thirst." He touched the screen of the menu-tab several times before setting it aside.

"Okay, and an arti-sour for me." She touched the menu-tab and looked at him intently.

Heart looked back at her and then cast a glance around the room. When he turned back, he saw she was still looking at him. "What?"

"We both seem to be outcasts."

"Speak for yourself. I'm a fun-loving guy who's the life of the party."

She smirked. "Oh, really now?"

"My lot in life isn't the best, but it isn't the worst. I've seen worse. I've seen dead, and I don't think you can get any worse than that. It wasn't my choice to end up in the settlements, but now that I've lived there, I look at it all as an education. It's opened my eyes to a different perspective on life. I can't help thinking my earlier life was closed and sheltered — sort of artificial. I like to think I value life more than I did before."

A waiter arrived, setting down their drinks and a sizzling wok with two plates and chopsticks. Heart picked up his glass and held it out. Stanton clinked her glass against his. "Cheers," he said, taking one of the plates and sliding the other across the table to Stanton.

"Thanks, but no thanks," she said.

"I ordered for two. I figured you'd change your mind, Sergeant."

"Call me Elizabeth."

He manipulated his chopsticks and picked up a beetle. "Tell me about yourself, Elizabeth. You said earlier you like the city and the finer things in life. Tell me about those."

"I don't want to be a cultural ignoramus. I'd like there to be more to me than just my job."

"Music. Do you play an instrument?"

"I took the usual piano lessons when I was a girl but never pursued it when I got to high school. You?"

"I've strummed a few guitar chords in my life."

The music changed to a slower number and more couples headed to the dance floor. Heart took a moment to watch the dancers.

"Do you dance?" Stanton asked.

"Why, thank you. Kind of you to ask." He stood up and put his hand out.

"No, I..." She stared at his hand, alarmed. "I don't dance."

"We all dance, Elizabeth. Let's take advantage of the moment."

"I don't know how, Matthew."

He took hold of her hand. "I'll teach you."

She sighed and put down her drink. Heart continued to hold her hand as they glided down the three steps to the dance floor. They squeezed between the couples and found a spot in the middle. He held her one hand up and used his other to guide her hand to his shoulder, sliding his hand around her waist as he did so. "The man always starts with his left because the woman is always right."

She chuckled. "Funny man. Maybe that drink has gone to my head. You never would have gotten me down here without it."

"Am I going to find myself disciplined for plying you with drink?"

"You're the charming rogue."

"Me? I'm an honorable gentleman."

"Let's see if I have to slap your hand."

Heart guided her through a series of steps, with a few missteps and apologies, ending the song with a slight bow. "Thank you."

A tango started and he cocked an ear. "That may be pushing our luck."

After returning to their table, they ordered a second round of drinks and finished the remaining food while sharing personal stories.

Stanton led Heart to his hotel room. "Here you go." She pressed her thumb to the scanner and held the door open.

He took a step forward, bumping into her. "Sorry."

They both moved in an attempt to get around the other, bumping into each other again. The two officers stood face-to-face. She gazed at his mouth. "I haven't been with a man in a while."

"Neither have I."

Her forehead creased in confusion, and then she laughed.

Heart moved closer and she stopped laughing. He leaned in, pressing his lips to hers. Stanton didn't flinch but stared wide-eyed down the corridor.

Heart backed away, and they studied one another inquisitively.

"Tomorrow at oh nine hundred," Stanton said.

"Yes."

"In the lobby of the MetPol."

"Yes."

"Thanks for the drink."

"You're welcome."

She turned and walked to the elevator. "Good night."

"Good night."

The doors opened, and she stepped inside.

Heart watched the doors close, staring down the now-empty hallway. It was late. He shut the door.

Chapter 8

Heart entered from the street and strode across the lobby to where Stanton was waiting.

"Detective Heart." She touched her ear-tab.

"Good morning," he said, smiling at her formality.

"I have arranged to meet with the head of SynthResearch at oh nine-thirty. I have a car outside."

He nodded. "I'm curious. Why do you use an ear-tab? I would have thought your personal display would be built-in."

"It is. But in public I find it easier to show a display to ward off inquisitive people. Otherwise they think I'm lost, staring into space."

Walking out the front doors, they headed toward a flivver parked at the curb.

"I want to apologize," she said suddenly.

"For what?"

"My behavior last night was unprofessional."

"Listen, Eliz—"

"Detective Heart, it won't happen again." She got in the car, leaving no room for argument.

He sighed and climbed in after her.

Stanton took them up to the main corridor before setting the autopilot. "John Eden has been the head of SynthResearch for the past five years. He has a PhD in both biotechnology and computer sciences. He's considered the foremost expert in all things relating to humans and machines. I heard him give a talk last year at a symposium on artificial intelligence. I've come to appreciate his talent as something of a miracle worker, given my situation. I wouldn't be alive if it weren't for him."

"Was Bachmann involved in the business?"

"He was the owner and the principal investor, but I don't know if he was involved in the business. Eden's the genius. I think Bachmann recognized it was a good investment — the way of the present and the way of the future."

"This may not lead to anything, but we have to explore all angles."

The car broke from the main flyway and veered off between two skyscrapers. It passed several towers before slowing at a landing entrance on the thirtieth floor of their destination. An illuminated sign read SynthResearch. They exited the car as the autopark took over.

They stared at a device hovering at eye level: a half-meter cube with rounded edges. It was a dull metallic gray with no distinguishing features.

"Sergeant Stanton. Detective Heart. MetPol officers," Stanton said.

"Follow me, please," the cube replied.

They followed as the cube glided into a waiting elevator. After a short ride, the number on the wall display changed from thirty to thirty-one, and the doors reopened. "Follow me, please." The cube exited and floated toward a woman sitting behind a reception desk. "Sergeant Stanton and Detective Heart to see Dr. Eden." The cube moved to one side.

The officers approached the desk. "Good morning," Stanton said.

The woman looked up, revealing that it was an android. Seams were visible on various parts of the body: on either side of the head, the neck, the interior and exterior of the arms, the shoulders, and the wrists. It spoke in a clipped monotone. "Good. Mor. Ning. Ser. Geant. Stan. Ton. One. Mo. Ment. Please. I. Will. An. Nounce. You." It touched an ear-tab. "Doc. Tor. E. Den. Your. Guests. Are. Here." It paused. "Yes. Sir."

The mechanical receptionist stood up and walked around the desk. "If. You. Would. Fol. Low. Me." Turning around, it walked toward a door and put a thumb on a wall scanner. The door slid open. "This. Way."

It led them across a spacious office. Behind a desk sat a man with his back to them, fiddling with a device on a credenza.

"Doc. Tor. E. Den. Your. Guests."

The man turned around and smiled. "That will be all, Rosie."

"Yes. Sir." The android withdrew from the office.

The doctor stood up and stuck out a hand. "Sergeant Stanton. Detective Heart. I'm John Eden. Chief Voynich said he would appreciate any help I could provide for your investigation." He pointed to some chairs. "Please, have a seat."

Eden sat down and leaned on his desk. "I was sorry to hear about Bachmann. This is a great loss loss. He was more than an investor — he was a great supporter of the work we do here here."

Stanton and Heart glanced at one another, wondering at the strange repetition.

"Thank you for your time, Dr. Eden," she said. "Is there anything out of the ordinary you could tell us about Willard Bachmann? Was he behaving differently as of late?"

"I couldn't say one way or another. I did not see the man on a regular basis basis. We spoke from time to time. However, he didn't didn't didn't come see me."

"Sir?"

"He would drop by once in a while to to to hear the latest news in our—"

Eden froze midsentence, mouth agape and arm arrested midgesture.

"—development. That man had a keen interest in bridging the gap between man and machine." Eden nodded in confirmation.

"Are you okay, sir?"

"Yes. Why why why do do you ask?"

"Well, sir..." Stanton stared at Eden, who was again frozen. "Is there something wrong with him?"

Heart stood and leaned over the desk, waving one hand in front of Eden's face. "He didn't blink. Has he had a seizure?"

The office door slid open. "Goddammit! We're never going to get this stupid thing to work."

Both Stanton and Heart looked over to see another John Eden enter the room. He marched up to his double behind the desk and slapped him on the side of the head. "Why do you ask?" the double repeated. He jerked, seeing Eden standing over him. "Uh-oh. Did I freeze again?"

Eden sighed. "Yes, you did." He turned to the officers. "I apologize. I couldn't resist doing a test run of our latest android, but I'm afraid the arti-brain is not yet meeting our standard." He patted the android on the shoulder. "Okay, John. That's enough for today. You can head back to the lab. I'll be down later to work out an assessment of today's run with Professor Delambre."

"O. O. O. Kay, Dr. Eden. Sorry about that that. I'm doing my best best." The android stood and left the office.

Eden sat, grinning. "Once again, I apologize. I get enthusiastic about my work and can't resist trying it out. I'm sure the unsuspecting public, such as yourselves, finds this eccentric. However, I hope you'll believe me when I say it's for a good cause."

"Sure." Heart gave an amused smile.

"It's the arti-brain. That's what stumps us. We've done wonderful, inventive things with every other part of the body: arms, hands, legs, heart, lungs, kidneys — well, you see where I'm going with this. But the brain? That's one complicated organ! Old science fiction kept talking about a positronic brain, an artificial brain capable of doing everything the real organ can do: think, remember, feel, imagine, even dream. So far, modern science hasn't been able to unlock the secret. Not only is the brain complicated, it's also a miniature computer. Despite our current nanotechnology, we can't shrink the necessary processing power down to the size of a human head. I think the best we could do is give you an android with a head the size of a beach ball. Quite out of proportion. As you can see with the android me, the head has limited functionality and is prone to problems. I suppose we could supplement brain power with a wireless connection to a central computer, but even then, we haven't arrived at an algorithm that mimics everything a human brain can do. Someday, at some point in the future, we'll have an arti-brain small enough to fit inside the space of a human skull and powerful enough to make you believe it's human."

"It's impressive, Dr. Eden." Heart rubbed his chin, trying to grasp the implications of this development.

"What's impressive, Detective Heart, is your partner." Eden smiled. "It's good to see you again, Elizabeth."

"Thank you, sir."

"Dr. Osler kept me in the loop about your case, and I must say the results were remarkable."

"I'm grateful for what you did for me."

"How are you doing in your new life?"

"I..." Her eyes darted toward Heart. "I'm fine, sir. Life isn't the same as I knew it, but it's good. I'm getting along well."

"Good. You're one of the few who point the way to the future. How can we extend humanity's reach by combining man and machine? How can we prolong life? We're at the frontier of science."

"Dr. Eden, I'd like to return to Willard Bachmann," Heart said.

"Yes. The reason for your visit."

"You said Bachmann had a keen interest in your business."

"Yes."

"Was Bachmann whole?"

"Yes, he was," Eden said. "However, he was not a narrow-minded thinker. Unlike some who hold deep-rooted prejudices, he thought the work we do complemented humanity — enhanced it. He thought what we were doing was the next step in humanity's evolution."

"Very philosophical," Heart said.

"I found him to be one of the more forward thinkers on the council."

"Oh?"

"Not all the members share the same enthusiasm for our work. Some look upon necrofasc with horror. A lack of understanding leads to baseless opinions and wild explanations, none founded in fact. People call it a problem of lifestyle or a problem of poverty. Some look at it as a problem of the ground. Some even go so far as to say it's retribution for sin. There's no end to what people think are legitimate causes of what is nothing more than mutated bacteria. Mutations happen all the time, but add on top of it an environment sullied by pollution, chemical waste, and nuclear fallout, and you have a crucible for the uncontrollable."

"Did Bachmann come here often?" Heart asked.

"Not to visit me, but he did come on a semi-regular basis to visit with our AI division. He and the director, Andre Delambre, were good friends."

"Would it be possible to meet with Professor Delambre?"

"By all means." Eden touched his ear-tab. "Toby? Would you come in here?"

The office door slid open as the hovering cube entered. "Yes, Dr. Eden? How may I be of service?"

"Would you escort Sergeant Stanton and Detective Heart to see Professor Delambre?"

"Yes, sir."

Eden stood up and shook hands. "If there's anything else I can do for you, please contact me at any time. I'd like to do whatever I can to assist in bringing the perpetrator to justice."

"Follow me," Toby said.

They took the elevator down to a workshop that took up an entire floor. Groups of people were working in discrete areas, surrounded by equipment and displays. There was a general hum of activity, conversations, and machines.

"Follow me."

They trailed the cube through a maze of tables until they came to a diminutive man with thick glasses, stooped over a workbench. He had both hands inside a cube.

"Professor Delambre, this is Sergeant Stanton and Detective Heart."

Without looking up, the professor said, "Thank you, Toby." He took both hands out of the cube, stared inside, and shrugged. "It'll have to do." He picked up a square piece of metal and set it on top of the cube, pushing down until there was a click. "I'm assuming you're here about Bachmann." He touched the front of the cube and it rose off the table. "I don't know anything."

A melodious female voice emanated from the device. "Good morning, Professor Delambre. How are you?"

"I'm fine, Kimberly. Are you ready for duty?"

"Yes, sir. All systems are functioning within normal parameters. I feel in tip-top condition."

"Good. Would you join Toby for today's test exercise in Lab Six?"

"Yes, sir."

"Follow me, Kimberly."

"Yes, Toby."

The humans watched the cubes float away.

Heart regarded the professor curiously. "Why is it that Toby and Kimberly have smooth speech, yet Rosie has a clipped pattern?"

"The cubes are connected to a central system. Their intelligence is not in the box itself — it comes from a supercomputer providing AI functionality. Rosie, however, is a self-contained arti-brain. She is state of the art and represents the limitations of our current technology. We've made great strides over the past few years, but that spark of consciousness, that essential part of what defines a sentient being, eludes us. Our AI is heuristic, granted, but it's not alive."

"I take it this was what fascinated Willard Bachmann."

"Bachmann was fond of puzzles, and heuristics is an extension of that process. He was an amateur, but a knowledgeable one. He had delved into various aspects of problem-solving and the attempts over the years to codify how we humans accomplish what we do. What interested him was the concept of thinking, the idea of consciousness. What makes us, us? He wanted to understand the essential elements of a human being. What differentiates us from bacteria? What differentiates us from a fish?"

"Has anybody answered that question, Professor Delambre?"

He shrugged. "We sometimes think we have, and other times it appears as if we aren't even close."

"Professor," Stanton said, "did Bachmann own any of your

technology?"

"He was whole, so he didn't need any of our prosths."

"Anything else?"

"We loaned him a hover cube a few months back. It amused him, but he didn't think it served any practical purpose in his day-to-day life."

"What about an android?"

"He never expressed much interest."

Stanton gestured to Heart. "Can you think of anything else?"

"Not at the moment," Heart said.

"Thank you for your time, Professor. We'll be in touch if we have any other questions."

The police officers headed back to the flivver.

"When Rupert said 'it,' what was he referring to?" Stanton said.

"I don't know." Heart paused. "I'm curious. Can Eden confirm what Delambre said?"

"Confirm what?"

"That Bachmann didn't own anything."

Stanton touched the dash-tab, activating the call. The screen cleared and the image of John Eden stared back.

"Dr. Eden, I apologize for the bother, but we have a question."

"Anything."

"Did Bachmann own any of your technology?"

"I don't know. A moment." Eden worked off-screen. "I see at various times we've loaned him items. This report says he had a hover cube a while back."

"Professor Delambre mentioned that."

Eden frowned. "Just a sec." He stared out of view. "Strange. Our records from two months ago show Marie Amble took possession of a Mark IV android. That's the same model you saw of me today."

"What's so odd about that?"

"Marie Amble is Willard Bachmann's partner."

***

"Delambre lied." Heart shifted in his seat as the auto-belt engaged.

Stanton set the car in motion. "Maybe he didn't know."

"Didn't know? It was a surprise birthday gift and he was sworn to secrecy?"

"Okay, when you put it that way."

"I don't think they're mass-producing androids, flying out the door by the hundreds. Delambre knew all right, and he lied to us."

"Should we bring him in for questioning?"

"I doubt that would lead to anything concrete at this stage of the game. Why don't we visit the partner and see if she knows anything?"

Stanton again touched the dash-tab, swiping through a menu. "Amble lives at the top of Tower One of The New Dakota in Central Park. We'll take the crosstown corridor and drop out at West Seventy-Second. We can park at Tower Two and take the skywalk across."

"Ah, how the other half lives."

"You mean the other half of the one percent."

Within thirty minutes they had crossed the glass-enclosed walkway joining the towers at the thirtieth floor and ridden up to the fortieth. The elevator exited into a small hallway with two doors, one marked with a nameplate showing Marie Amble. Stanton touched the wall-tab.

A middle-aged woman in a pantsuit opened the door. "Yes?"

"Ms. Amble?"

"Yes?"

"I'm Sergeant Stanton with the MetPol. This is Detective Heart. May we come in and ask you a few questions about Willard Bachmann?"

"What?" Amble glanced back in the apartment. "I wasn't expecting—"

"This won't take long."

"I was busy."

"We won't take up much of your time, Ms. Amble. Your input may assist with our investigation."

Amble bit her lip. "All right. I guess." She backed away from the door.

"Thank you."

Amble shut the door behind the officers and led them into a large room with several couches. "Please, have a seat." Stanton sat while Heart remained standing and looked around.

"How may I help you?"

"What was the nature of your relationship with Willard Bachmann?"

"That's personal."

"This is a murder investigation."

Amble's gaze darted around. "We were seeing one another."

"For how long?"

"It had been some time."

"How long, approximately?"

"Three months? Four?"

"You weren't married."

"That's correct. Both of us had been married and divorced. We were shy about taking such a drastic next step."

Heart wandered over to a sizable window overlooking Central Park. He gazed out at the well-planned but natural expanse of trees and bushes, interrupted by open grass and ponds. "You have a beautiful view, Ms. Amble."

"Thank you, Detective Heart. I'm lucky to have landed this apartment. Such gems are a rarity."

Leaning toward the glass, he looked left and then right. "I'm curious."

"Pardon?"

Heart turned around to face her. "Could you explain why there is a flivver parked outside?"

Amble stiffened. "The building management was washing the exterior windows. I suppose it's for the maintenance man."

"Would you mind if I take a look?"

"I guess not." Amble glanced around again. "I mean, no. Go ahead."

Heart crossed the room and passed through a large archway, which led into a dining area. He touched a wall-tab and the glass door to the balcony slid open. Stepping out, he leaned on the railing to look down at the hovering vehicle. It was black, with no distinguishing marks. He touched his ear-tab to open the display. "Identify." The system showed no match. "Transponder." Not functioning. He crouched down and looked through the barrier at the side of the car. There were scratches on the side. "Mike Alfa Charlie, dash two-five-six India Echo Echo Echo." A sixty-four-digit hexadecimal number scrolled by. "Create Folder. Bachmann. Save."

He stood up. "Call Stanton." There was a beep, and he spoke in a low voice. "Don't acknowledge I'm talking to you. I believe this is the car we saw the other night. No markings. No transponder. I think I can see scratches on the side. Somebody may be in Amble's apartment, but I don't know if she is aware."

Walking back inside, Heart shut the door. The two women continued to talk as he glanced out the window before looking around the dining room. He made a note of various doors connecting to other parts of the penthouse and then walked back into the living room.

"Did you see what you wanted, Detective Heart?"

"Yes, thank you."

"Was it the maintenance staff?"

"It would seem so. Does this penthouse take up the entire floor, Ms. Amble?"

"Just half. I share the fortieth story with Charles and Nancy Hathaway — a charming couple, both in their seventies. Would you like a tour of the penthouse?"

"That would be most kind of you."

"Let me take you into the den. I'm proud of having a functioning fireplace." Amble got up and pointed. "This way."

Stanton and Heart shot one another a glance. Heart peeked back toward the living room as they advanced into the hallway.

"My husband strived for a rich, warm atmosphere. While actual wood was not always available, there are modern substitutes indistinguishable from the real thing. One must make do with what one has."

Amble took them through the various rooms, showing off pieces of furniture and artwork, before arriving back at the living room. "I'm sorry, I wandered off on a tangent, but I find this apartment is enjoyable. Is there anything else I can help you with?"

"I don't think so, Ms. Amble. You've been most helpful." Stanton stood. "Heart? Anything else?"

He was again standing by the window, looking out. "Yes. One other thing." He turned and snapped. "Two months ago, you took possession of a Mark IV android. Why? And where is it?"

She stood still, her eyes vacant.

"Ms. Amble?"

She opened her mouth and then closed it.

"You needn't worry. He's gone," Heart said.

Amble cleared her throat. "I'm going to ask you to leave now."

"We can take you in for questioning."

"You have no right. I want to call my lawyer."

"As you wish, Ms. Amble," Heart said. "But I would like to remind you that you may be protecting a murderer."

"I have nothing further to say."

She led the officers out, and they took the elevator back down to the thirtieth floor.

"Somebody was there," Heart said.

"What makes you say that?"

"She was nervous, even defensive. The story about maintenance was a cover. A maintenance car would have specific markings. That one had none. And a non-functioning transponder? No way. On top of it all, after her tour of the apartment, the mysterious flivver was gone. She led us around to give whoever it was a chance to slip out. Somebody was definitely there."

"Who?" Stanton asked.

"I have no idea. But, considering Rupert's mention of an 'it' and this unaccounted-for android, I'm wondering if they are not the same thing."

"If there was somebody in the apartment, do you think it could have been the android?"

"From what we saw at SynthResearch, I don't see how an android would be sophisticated enough to function on its own. It wouldn't get far, undetected in society. Its odd speech patterns would make it stand out in a crowd."

They sat in their flivver, both deep in thought.

Heart turned to Stanton. "What do we know about Bachmann and Amble?"

Stanton touched the dash-tab. "Marie Amble, fifty-eight years old. PhD in philosophy, and professor at New York University for twenty years. Married at twenty-nine for fifteen years. Divorced. No children. Shrewd investor, independently wealthy, retired at forty-six."

She swiped to another screen. "Bachmann, fifty-six years old. Born Barbara Barres. Transitioned at nineteen. Changed name when mother remarried. MBA, top of his class. A whiz kid in business. Amassed a fortune buying up smaller, lackluster firms and turning them into profitable enterprises. Married at forty-one for eight years. Divorce amicable."

Heart closed his eyes and massaged his forehead.

"Hmm, there's a medical addendum," Stanton said.

"What's it say?"

"I don't see anything. It's empty."

"Why would somebody create an addendum and not put anything in it?"

"I see no security restrictions."

"Did somebody erase it?"

"I can't tell."

"Is there anything in the file about his health, like the name of his doctor? There's got to be somebody we can go see."

She swiped the dash-tab again. "It says Dr. Joseph McGaugh of the Center for Neural Science."

"Isn't that a research facility?"

"Yes."

"Wouldn't his doctor be a GP? Why would he be seeing a specialist?"

"I don't know."

"Let's find out."

Chapter 9

The rotund man smiled at his unexpected visitors. "Good afternoon. How odd to have the police making inquiries. Have a seat."

"Dr. McGaugh, we'll try not to take up too much of your time," Stanton said, introducing herself and Heart.

"I'm listening."

"Willard Bachmann was seeing you."

"Yes. Still is. My calendar shows an appointment next week."

"He won't make it," Stanton said.

"Oh?"

"You haven't seen the news?"

"Sorry, I'm out of touch, with work and such." McGaugh motioned to his desk, which was overflowing with files. "I don't follow the everyday gossip of the public. There's more than enough here to keep me occupied."

"Willard Bachmann is dead."

"Dead? But this is unexpected. In fact, this is impossible! I was positive our treatment had stabilized his condition."

"What condition was that, Doctor?"

"Willard came to me about six months ago on a referral from his own GP. He'd become concerned about lapses in memory, confusion in his daily life. His physician didn't know what to do, so he sent him to me. I did a battery of tests and discovered Willard was suffering from a rare form of necrofasc, a type of Creutzfeldt-Jakob disease."

"Sorry, Doctor," Stanton said. "Please explain."

"It's a degenerative neurological disease that's considered incurable and fatal, but recent breakthroughs have proven promising in stopping its advancement and leaving the patient in partial remission. I had high hopes for Willard. This is an unfortunate turn of events."

"It is," Stanton said. "Willard Bachmann was murdered."

"What?"

"Do you know of anybody who would want to see him

dead?" she asked.

"I don't know. Our relationship was strictly medical."

"You knew who he was."

"Of course. I may not follow the headlines on a regular basis, but I'm aware of politics. As a research facility we rely on funding. Some of it is private, but most comes from the government, and we pay close attention to our relationships with the powers that be."

"If we could come back to your diagnosis. How did Bachmann take the news?"

"Well..." The doctor paused, considering something. "He was upset when he first came to me and was diagnosed. Who wouldn't be, considering it was a death sentence? However, I thought he seemed buoyed by the remission. He was suffering from the first symptoms of the disease, but it wasn't getting worse."

"These first symptoms," Stanton said, "how severe were they? Were they incapacitating?"

"Not completely. We've all had our moments — forgetting things, not understanding situations or people — but we recover, as these events are almost always due to our being distracted. We're not paying attention. Willard, however, reported being unable to recover. He had escalating occurrences of forgetfulness about normal, everyday things. At times, he would be unable to follow a conversation, even if he was familiar with the topic. He knew he wasn't behaving normally."

"You said this treatment put him in partial remission."

"Yes," McGaugh said. "We felt the symptoms wouldn't worsen."

"But he would still have to deal with the symptoms he was already experiencing."

"Yes."

"So, he wouldn't get worse, but he wouldn't get better."

McGaugh nodded. "Yes, that's what I'm saying."

"You said he seemed buoyed by the news."

"I suppose. However, I wonder if it wouldn't be more

accurate to say he wasn't so upset anymore."

"Was he ever upset after the start of treatment?" Stanton asked.

"Oh, there were times he was agitated. He told me he looked at this as being a slow and painful death."

"Would you label him as desperate?"

"I suppose. Who wouldn't be?" McGaugh shrugged.

"Did Bachmann consult with anybody else, like a therapist?"

"He never mentioned anyone like that, but I remember him saying a few times that his partner was distraught. He wondered if she distanced herself from him because she couldn't deal with his disease."

Stanton glanced at Heart but he said nothing, listening intently.

"Doctor, I thank you for your time." She stood up. "If you think of anything else, please give us a call."

A few minutes later, they were crossing the lobby of the research facility.

"I need to visit the men's room," Heart said.

"Fine, I'll wait over there."

He walked down a short hall, entered the restroom, and stood at a urinal to do his business. Lost in thought, he was only vaguely aware of the door opening and the sound of approaching footsteps. He was zipping himself up when a voice said, "Matthew Heart?"

"Yes?"

Two hands grabbed him roughly by the lapels and lifted him off the floor. They swung him sideways and pushed him up against a wall, his feet dangling. "Shit!" Heart, shocked, looked down at the man's face.

"Stay away," the man said.

"What?" Heart managed to grab hold of the man's hands and tried to pull them apart.

"Stay away or else."

"Who the hell are you?" Heart struggled and kicked, but the man held fast.

"I will stop you."

Heart clenched his fist and struck the man on the cheek. The man's head tilted, but he remained unfazed by the punch. Still holding Heart by the lapels, he half threw, half pushed him across the room. Heart slammed into the far wall, groaning in pain.

The man came at Heart and wound up for a punch, but Heart ducked and the man's fist smashed through the tiled wall. As the assailant struggled to disengage his hand, the detective ran out the door into the hall, tripped, and crashed into the opposite wall. A hand seized his jacket collar, pulling him up. Heart saw a fist arcing toward his face when another hand grabbed his attacker's wrist, stopping it midflight.

"You're under arrest for assaulting a police officer," Stanton said.

The man dropped Heart and threw a punch with his free hand, which Stanton also blocked. Pushing forward, he managed to slam her against the wall. Stanton jammed her unoccupied hand against his face, shoving his head backward. With a sudden movement, he broke free, seized her by the shoulders, and threw her across the corridor.

The man then lunged at Stanton, but she hit him with a right hook. He blinked and she hit him again. As he raised a fist to strike, she pivoted and hit him, mid-chest, with a back kick. The man flew backward and lay sprawled out on the floor. With a quick glance at Stanton, he scrambled to his feet and ran down the hall.

Stanton rushed over and grabbed hold of Heart's arm. "You okay?"

"Go! Go get him!"

Hurriedly, the two followed down the hall and burst through a door marked Exit. Finding themselves on the street, they scanned the area for the culprit.

"There!" Heart pointed and started sprinting. They dodged several pedestrians, trying to keep their eyes on their quarry as he darted into the research center's parking garage. They stopped short at the entrance. An automated valet service parked cars on several levels using an elevator. The front area was empty and the elevator was closed, but the door to the staircase was just shutting.

The officers charged up the stairs, their footsteps echoing in the concrete stairwell. Two flights up, another door was closing. Heart yanked it open and ran out, looking one way, then the other. Nothing was there but dozens of parked flivvers. It was quiet. Whispering to Stanton, he said, "You go left. I'll go right."

They separated, stooping down to look under the parked vehicles. Moving into the next row of cars, Heart crouched down when he heard a whirring noise from behind. He sprang to one side, rolling to safety as a flivver barreled down the main aisle toward a massive window between two support columns. It crashed through the glass and disappeared into the busy flyway.

A horn honked. "Get in!" Stanton yelled. Heart leaped up and into the passenger seat of their police flivver as she slapped a flashing light on the roof and hit the siren. Roaring down the row of cars, they flew through the broken window.

"He went right." Heart pointed, and his partner headed off in pursuit. "Who the hell was that guy? I thought he was going to murder me."

"I think you answered your own question." Stanton said, scanning the cross flyways. "I'm assuming he's our murderer." She veered around a slow flivver and spoke into the dash-tab. "Call Central. Officer Stanton, Badge #4711. In pursuit of a black sedan on East Twenty-Ninth Street, heading west. Suspect is a synth. Proceed with extreme caution. Suspect is violent."

"What? A synth?"

"You didn't think he tossed you around like a rag doll because he visits the gym each day, did you? If he had punched you, you'd be dead right now."

The suspect's flivver turned left on Fifth Avenue and headed south. Stanton kept a wide margin between them and regular traffic. "This guy's crazy. He doesn't care what happens. We're either going to kill somebody, get ourselves killed, or both."

"Don't slow down! Keep going!" Heart leaned forward, pointing at the suspect's car ahead.

"What the hell happened back there?"

"I don't know. I went to the men's room, and that guy must have come in after me. He manhandled me, pushing me against the wall, and said to stay away. No, he said, 'Stay away or else.' Or else what? Kill me?"

"That's all?"

"No. After that he said he would stop me. Stop me from what, I don't know. I punched him, but he barely flinched."

As they went into a turn, Stanton was forced to rise above a truck before descending back onto their route.

"A synth is completely artificial," she said. "Their overall strength is four or five times that of a human. A person with a prosth arm has increased strength in their arm, but it's still only as strong as the body to which it is attached. Even if the arm can support a heavy weight, the rest of the body can't. A synth is stronger because everything — arms, torso, and legs — is all artificial."

The suspect swerved off at an angle and careened over Madison Square Park, taking out two kites and a remote-controlled model flivver.

"Shit," Heart said.

The car veered east on Twenty-Third Street, shooting up thirty stories to a clear fly level.

"When I returned to training after my transition, I had to learn how to pull my punches. I couldn't go all out while sparring, as I could seriously hurt somebody, even maim or kill them." Stanton steered around another slow-moving car.

"So, this guy is not your normal bad guy." Heart braced himself between the door and the console as they continued the high-speed chase.

"Everything is synth: arti-vision and arti-hearing. He'll have the built-in functionality I have. Your ear-tab gives you a similar range of enhancements to your senses, as well as provides communication."

"I wonder who he is."

"There are few synths. In fact, they're rare. Very rare. The science is specialized and brand new. I'm sure we could track down names and end up with a number small enough that we could check them ourselves."

"First on the list should be Delambre," Heart said. "He lied to us, and I'd like to find out why."

The suspect's flivver swooped over FDR Drive and dove over the east side of the metrofloat.

A synthesized voice called out from the dashboard, "Eastern border. Eastern border. Too fast. Unauthorized exit."

Stanton flew over the edge and rolled over, pointing the vehicle straight down. Disoriented, Heart gasped. "Whoa!" The panorama of surrounding skyscrapers exploded into the broad expanse of plains a kilometer below.

"Where's he going?" Stanton yelled.

A warning buzzer sounded. "Warning! Warning! Impact in five hundred meters!"

Stanton braked and pulled the flivver out of its descent.

Heart gestured to the right. "Over there! Over there!"

She sped toward a small shack in the middle of a field. The suspect had exited his flivver and was running away. "Where the hell does he think he's going?" Stanton said, setting their flivver down beside the suspect's vehicle. "Where'd he go?"

They scanned the apparently empty field.

"There!" Heart pointed and broke into a run.

"Where?" Stanton ran after him.

"Over there. I see an open hatch to an irrigation tunnel."

"Pardon?"

"There are underground feeder canals for moving large quantities of water from rivers to dry areas. These places are flat, so there are pumping stations to keep the water flowing."

"He climbed inside one?"

"Some tunnels are big enough for a flivver."

Heart rushed to the hatch and stuck his head in the opening. "I can hear someone running." He pivoted and put one foot on the top rung of a ladder.

Stanton grabbed his arm. "Let me go first. If there's trouble, I want to meet him head-on."

"Okay."

She scrambled down and Heart soon followed. The bottom of the ladder ended at another open hatch in the side of the tunnel. They stared down the irrigation pipe, which was illuminated by recessed emergency lights every hundred meters. The sound of running feet was faint.

"Where's he going?" Stanton whispered.

"To the next maintenance hatch."

"How far is that?"

"Depends. Could be half a kilometer or a kilometer. I think it varies according to the branches of the distribution system."

At a loss, they stood looking down the dimly lit pipe.

"Now what?"

"We can't catch him on foot. Let's go back up and ride down to the next hatch. He's got to surface at some point."

Stanton spun around. "Did you hear something?"

"Hear what?" Heart turned and looked up the tunnel.

"Why is the wind picking up?"

As they listened, there was a growing rumble. The distant emergency lights were blinking out, one by one.

"Holy shit! The sluice gates have been opened and the tunnel's filling with water. Get up! Now!"

Heart shoved Stanton out the side hatch and pushed her toward the ladder. He reached through and grabbed the first rung with one hand when a surge of water swept him off his feet. Thrashed about, his hand clasped the first thing it found: Stanton's ankle. As the water rose over his head, a hand grasped his forearm and hauled him into the access tube. The pressure of the current propelled them up the length of the ladder and they burst out of the hatch, tumbling to the ground. Stanton pressed a panel and the gushing water subsided.

Standing, Heart slapped dirt off his soaked clothes. "That was close."

"Too close. I believe our suspect was hoping we would run

after him. We would have been swept away with no chance of escape."

"I think you're right. This guy is ruthless." Heart shook out his jacket. "Crap, I'm soaked."

"My uniform is made from waterproof materials. It doesn't absorb liquids."

"Lucky you."

A shadow passed over as they talked, and they both looked up. The metrofloat had drifted overhead, blocking the sun.

"Let's walk back to the suspect's flivver. I'll dry out a bit, and we can check for clues."

"Okay."

They had just set off when Heart stopped. "Just a second." Holding onto Stanton's arm, he raised one foot and took off his shoe. He tipped it over and water poured out. "Ugh. I feel icky." He switched hands and repeated the action for the other shoe.

A horn sounded overhead. Stanton looked up. "What's that?"

They gazed at the underside of the metrofloat, a kilometer above. The details were indistinct, but they could make out the machinery, catwalks, and piping of the city's supporting infrastructure.

The horn sounded again.

"I've never seen the city from this vantage point," Stanton said. "It's huge."

Looking around, Heart glanced up at the floating city and scowled.

"What's the matter?" she asked, noticing the look.

The horn now wailed in one-second intervals.

"Oh, crap." He sprinted toward the shack where they had parked the flivver. "Run! Run!"

She darted after him. "What? What's going on?"

The horn let out one long blast as he reached the structure and fumbled with the door latch. "Goddammit."

"What's the problem?"

Finally managing to get the door open, Heart pulled her

inside. "Do you have any idea how much waste thirty million people produce?" he asked, yanking the door shut and checking the latch.

"Uh, no."

He went to a window and looked outside, gesturing for her to come stand beside him. "Break waste into its components: garbage and sewage. They recycle just about everything, and I mean everything."

Stanton looked out the window, not comprehending.

"What do you think they do with all that sewage?"

"I know it's used for fertilizer."

"And how do you think they get what's up there down here?"

A pinging noise sounded on the roof of the shack.

"Fecal sludge is broken down, processed, and then sprayed onto fields." He pointed outside. "Like I said, everything is recycled. Nothing is wasted."

Several loud thumps rang out as the roof shook.

"Although, not all sewage falls like rain," he said. "There can be the occasional, uh, chunks."

There was now sporadic plopping sounds as blobs of fecal matter splattered to the ground.

"I've never seen this…"

"Floaters are ignorant of what goes on elsewhere. They don't understand how the city works."

"How do you know about this?"

"Years ago I worked in the fields, back when I knew nothing about farming. I was caught out in the open during a dump."

"A dump?"

"An appropriate name, I'd say. If getting soaked is icky, imagine getting soaked in sewage. I think I showered five times that day."

Stanton chuckled.

"You think that's funny?" He smirked. "Don't forget our flivver is being rained on."

She opened her mouth, stopped, and turned back to the

window.

Heart sniffed the air. "This is going to be an unpleasant experience."

The shower stopped, and the muffled sound of a long horn blast rang out.

"It's over." He negotiated around tools and equipment to look out another window. "It's safe to go outside." Opening the door, they ventured out. The ground was damp, the air humid.

Heart held his nose as he looked at their car. "We're covered in sh—"

"The suspect's car is gone."

He looked around, confirming her observation. "I bet he retrieved it by remote control. He ran down to the next maintenance hatch and called for his flivver."

"Was this dump, as you called it, a diversion?"

"Well, it kept us occupied while he made his getaway." Heart unspooled a hose from the side of the building. "The opening of the sluice gates, the dump. It's too much of a coincidence. I suspect our guy has security clearance for all areas of the city. There's no telling what operations he can override for his own benefit." He walked around their car, spraying it thoroughly.

"He's clever."

"I'll label this as more than clever. He has access to resources your normal bad guy doesn't." He opened the driver's door. "Get in, but let me spray your shoes. Let's not track this mess into our car."

Stanton went to the door and held up one foot. Heart cleaned it and she climbed halfway in before holding up the other foot, which he sprayed as well.

Pulling the hose around to the other side, he took care of his own shoes as he got in. Heart dropped the hose to the ground and closed his door. "Let's get back to the city and see if we can find out who our mysterious assailant is."

Chapter 10

"You're going to explain to me why you drove through the downtown core like a pair of lunatics." Voynich settled back in his desk chair.

"Sir, I was the one who initiated the pursuit. Heart had nothing to do with it." Stanton stood at attention, eyes forward.

"I have half a dozen reports from various squad cars about you hitting over one hundred twenty kilometers an hour. There were calls from the public about your fly over the park. I suppose it's a miracle you didn't have an accident." Voynich looked sternly at Heart.

Heart simply shrugged his shoulders.

"Sit down. This isn't a reprimand." Voynich sighed. "In the future, be more judicious about getting into high-speed chases. Invariably, they end badly and not always for the bad guy."

"Yes, sir," Stanton said.

"So, you're convinced our suspect is a synth."

"Yes, sir."

"Your report states Bachmann may have got his hands on an android."

"Yes, sir."

"An android isn't a synth." Voynich glanced at his desk-tab.

"No, sir."

"Is that all you're going to say, Sergeant?"

"Yes, sir. I mean no, sir. I—"

"What do you make of this, Heart?"

Heart tapped his chin in reflection. "I'm not sure. We're missing pieces of the puzzle."

"Speculate."

"Delambre lied to us. Amble lied to us. These people may be working together in a larger conspiracy. They're covering something up, but what that is we don't yet know. Bachmann was seeing a specialist who said his patient had an incurable disease and was dying. That makes me think Bachmann planned his death. It may have been suicide."

"He had himself murdered? How would that fit into any of this?"

"I don't know. If any of us found out we were going to die, what would we do? How would we plan our remaining days?"

Voynich looked at Stanton. "How many synths are there?"

"SynthResearch, the company that made me, has produced three in total. There are three other companies with similar technology. I could make a wild guess by multiplying three by four for twelve, but I would have to make inquiries to give you an accurate answer."

"Why a synth and not an android?"

"From what I understand, the current development of artificial brains is limited. Nothing yet rivals the human one. Androids, with their arti-brains, serve a purpose. However, for a brain capable of thought, reasoning, and even emotion, the best choice is a human one."

"Who would do such a thing? Who would give up their human body?"

"I doubt anybody would do it voluntarily, sir. In my case, I had no choice. My body was so badly damaged I would have died. Anybody else would only replace what was needed. Nobody would give up a working limb or organ. I assume Detective Heart would back me up on this, considering his experiences in the settlements."

"Heart?"

"I would say that's an accurate assessment of the situation. Although, in the settlements, due to lack of finances, many suffer from inferior prosths. Some can't afford a prosth at all and must make do without. Spending your life on crutches isn't much fun."

"What's next for your investigation?"

"I'd like to go back to Delambre and see if we can find out what he may be hiding."

"Fair enough. Anything else?"

"There's the question of this mystery man who came out of nowhere and threatened me. Is he getting desperate? Are we closing in? Is there a chance he may do something else?"

"Like make a mistake?" Voynich eyed Heart.

"I was thinking more like him going on the offensive."

"I have teams staying around the clock with Okafor and Enapay."

"No offense to you or your teams, but is it enough? This guy has proven himself to be skillful. He's circumvented security systems and remained incognito. Plus, he has access to specialized equipment. Never mind decapitating a body. Where does one get the equipment to extract a brain from the cranium?"

"True."

"And I don't think your average person has an electromagnetic pulse gun to knock autocabs out of the sky."

Voynich shifted in his chair. "Where would anybody get such stuff? They would have to have access to one of the specialty companies dealing in the technology research connected to military and policing."

"As I suggested before, one member of the council trying to take over may not be the right angle. It could be a second-in-command who has their eyes on power."

"Any ideas?"

"You know Charlie Vance is now working for Ashaki Okafor."

"Yes."

"He's a nasty bit of work," Heart said. "What he did to me aside, think about what he's doing to an entire settlement."

"Would he orchestrate such a maneuver?"

"I can't speak for his capabilities, but I know his motives."

"I did some investigation back when you two had your problems. There was nothing of interest. I recently pulled his file and, once again, nothing came up. I can't help thinking he may have connections in the force."

"Ever considered your office might be bugged?"

"I had this office swept after your report on the Singh bug. Nothing. However, coming back to Vance and his connections, when it comes to your problems and the problems at the settlement, he must have people on the payroll who are complicit in his dealings. We don't know what he's involved with here on the metrofloat."

With nothing more to discuss, the detectives took their leave and requisitioned a squad car.

"I've discovered Delambre didn't show up for work today," Stanton said. "Nobody knows where he is, so I got his home address. Let's see what we can find out."

They rode across town in silence, but after a few minutes Stanton made a slight noise.

"You have to clear your throat? I would have thought you didn't need to do that."

"No. I... Force of habit."

"You have something to say?"

"No."

"I'm listening."

"I wasn't going to say anything."

"Suit yourself." Heart looked out the window.

"It's difficult."

"Is it ever easy? But we can never forget our humanity."

"Are we talking about the same thing?" she asked.

"I don't know. What are you talking about?"

"What are you talking about?"

Both stared ahead. Heart glanced down at the console separating their seats, on which they each had a hand resting. He raised his little finger and brushed it against her hand.

She recoiled in alarm. "What the hell do you think you're doing?"

He suppressed a grin.

"I should punch you in the nose, Detective Heart." Her voice resonated with annoyance. "Oh, I get it, this is you playing the charming rogue."

"Sooner or later, you have to take a chance."

"Shaddup." She put both hands on the wheel and faced forward, the corners of her mouth turned up with the hint of a smile.

***

"Officer Stanton, Badge #4711. Request for security access. Andre Delambre, Hamilton Heights, citizen ID Papa Echo seven-nine-three." The door slid open as she put her thumb on the scanner.

They looked into the semi-darkness of the apartment. It was quiet. "Professor Delambre?" They looked at one another, apprehensive. "Professor Delambre?" Stanton unholstered her weapon and moved forward. She touched a wall-tab and the hallway lit up. They crept down the length of the corridor, stopping before a sizable open-concept room. There was a thump from behind and Heart whipped around, pulling his gun out of his shoulder holster and pointing it into the corner. A cat looked up at him and meowed.

Stanton pressed another wall-tab. "Look."

He turned back and saw a body crumpled on the floor. The face was smashed in.

"I assume that's the professor," she said. "That's what you would look like if I hadn't stopped our assailant."

"Shit."

"Officer Stanton, Badge #4711. Request forensics."

Stanton walked to a wall panel and repeated her badge number. "Request security logs."

Heart walked over and looked at the screen.

Stanton pointed at some figures. "Delambre opened his door at twenty hundred hours last night. He opened it again at twenty-two thirty. The lobby recorder shows no one coming in or going out between the hours of twenty-one hundred and twenty-three fifty. However, there was a security override on the rear fire exit at twenty-two twenty-five, and again twenty minutes later."

"The professor knew his murderer," Heart said.

"So it would seem."

"Maybe he was working with somebody and that person decided the professor was dispensable."

"What benefit would they see in his death?"

"His silence."

"But they must know we'd do a memory reconstruction."

"Yes, that's curious. If somebody's gone to all this trouble so far, why would they run such a risk? Are they getting careless? Or are they getting desperate? Desperation can lead to carelessness."

***

Back at HQ, Stanton walked up to the lab station with Heart in tow. "What do you have, Jake?"

"The trauma is significant. The frontal sinus has been pushed back as far as the pons. Parts of the mandible have touched the cerebellum, meaning the force of the blow was tremendous. I don't know what blunt instrument could have done this."

"I believe it was a fist."

"What?"

"We think a synth punched the professor."

"One punch?"

"Yes."

Jake shook his head in amazement. "In any case, we did complete anterior–posterior scans and then set surface probes to give ourselves a baseline as to what was there and what wasn't. We drilled through various points of the cranium to set up several BCI contacts, which we recorded and then reconstituted whatever engrams we could find. We verified the reliability of our recordings and constructed the following memories as of twenty-two thirty last night. Watch."

The three of them observed Delambre's point of view. He walked down the hall and turned to the wall-tab beside his apartment door. Touching the panel, the red for Locked changed to green for Unlocked. After, he walked back to the kitchen, got a glass out of the cupboard, ran the water, filled the glass, and drank. As he set the glass on the counter, the view rose to the ceiling, as if Delambre had been picked up off the ground. There were muffled cries and a voice said, "I will stop you."

Still showing the ceiling, they watched from Delambre's point of view as he was carried from the kitchen into the living room. There were more indistinct cries and a repetition of "I will stop you." This time it was stated more emphatically.

The professor was let go and he stumbled as he regained his footing. "What in God's name are you doing? Your secret is safe." Delambre turned to face the intruder and said, "I haven't told—" The display went black.

"Can you back it up, Jake?"

"Sure."

"Go slow. Can we see the attacker? Can we get a clear image?"

"I'll move forward frame by frame. Tell me which one you want."

Individual frames passed one by one until Stanton exclaimed, pointing at the display. "There! Who's that? Try the next frame." The display switched. "No, go back. I think that one is better. Can you enhance it?"

Jake fiddled with a hand-tab.

"What do you think, Heart?" Stanton eyed him.

"That's the guy."

"Jake, do a facial and compare."

"This could take a while," Jake said.

"We're not going anywhere."

The display changed, now showing an ongoing search for a facial match in the MetPol systems.

Heart scratched his temple. "I suspect a match isn't going to turn up."

"Why do you say that?" Stanton asked.

"Are synths registered?"

"Everybody has to be registered."

"Everybody. Except..."

"Except who?"

"Except the bad guys," Heart said.

"Funny."

"Your face is a synth face."

"Yes. It was designed from photos of my old face."

"Could you have asked for something else? A different face?"

"I suppose."

"What would happen if you damaged this face?"

"I would get it repaired," Stanton said.

"Or you could get a new one."

"Well, yes."

"Could a synth have multiple faces to appear as different people while in public?"

Stanton scrunched up her face, considering the possibility.

"I knew a farmer who had a specialty prosth with various tool attachments. At home, he had a normal arti-arm. But on the job, he'd switch to a special prosth to which he could attach various power tools to drill, saw, or bolt. If you can switch an arm, why not a face?"

"You're saying—"

"If you have a reason, you'll do it. The face we're looking at may not be the only face our perp is using. And since he knows we now know what he looks like, he could change it."

Heart tapped Jake on the shoulder. "Could you do another lookup for me?"

"Sure, what do you have?"

"I've got a MAC two-fifty-six address I took off a flivver during the course of our investigation. It may be nothing, but it won't hurt to have a look."

"Sure. Give me the transfer."

Heart flipped through his ear-tab folders and located the correct one. "Transfer."

"Got it."

"Any estimate of the time necessary?"

"This will be a snap." Jake poked at his hand-tab several times, swiping a finger across the screen. "Flivver, black sedan, two-door model. Manufactured two years ago."

"Current owner?"

"WillMar Industries. It's a company vehicle."

"And what, pray tell, is WillMar Industries?"

The lab attendant touched the display several times. "It's

involved in military development. They provide support to MetPol."

"Who owns the company?" Heart asked.

"Hmm, this says the company was founded by Willard Bachmann and Marie Amble."

"Willard and Marie," Stanton chimed in. "Are we getting warm?"

"I think, Sergeant Stanton," Heart said, "that we have given ourselves a new lead to chase down."

A buzzer sounded. "No match," Jake said. "This face isn't in MetPol's database. However, keep in mind we don't have everybody. ID chips are mandatory for all births on the metrofloat, but the settlements are another thing. On top of that, despite mandatory programs for ID recertification for adults, including photographs, people slip through. We have a lot, but we don't have everyone."

"Thanks, Jake. I'm not surprised. This is an unusual case, so it's to be expected. Our mysterious assailant gets even more so."

Chapter 11

On the front of the building, a story-high display alternated between the name WillMar Industries and pictures of happy people, with the scrolling catchphrase, Keeping the World Safe. Heart and Stanton had an appointment with Samuel Cummings, chief operations officer.

"Willard Bachmann was a good man and an excellent businessman. I appreciated the opportunity to work with him and was impressed at how he started this company from nothing and built it into one of the major players, if not the most important player, in the arms industry."

"Had you noticed any changes in his behavior as of late?"

Cummings shrugged. "Willard was a private man. I didn't know him at all outside work. However, over the past two years, he was transitioning himself away from the day-to-day operations. He hired me to deal with operations. He was still involved in the major decisions, the strategic direction of the corporation, but he was going to leave the running of the company up to me."

"Do you have a black sedan?"

"Me personally, or the company?"

"The company."

"It is our standard company car. We have a number of them. Why?"

"During our investigation, we ran across a flivver whose ID traced back to your company. We want to find out if there's any connection."

"If you give me the ID I can see what's in our records." He touched a hand-tab. "Lucy, would you come in here please?"

The office door opened and an android walked over to the desk. "Yes, Mr. Cummings? How may I be of service?"

"These people have the ID of one of our company cars. Would you find out where it's assigned?"

"Yes, sir." Lucy turned to Stanton. "If you would give me the transfer."

"Done."

"Searching." She looked at Cummings. "That car is assigned to Patrick Klint."

Cummings frowned. "Who's that?"

"He works at the Homey Testing Facility."

Cummings glanced at Stanton. "My apologies. We have so many employees, I don't know everybody by name."

"What's Homey?"

"It's an off-float area we use to test armaments. We can only do so much here in the city, so, for public safety, we work in the desert, well away from civilization, to ensure no one inadvertently gets hurt."

"Could we meet with this gentleman?"

"By all means. Lucy, where is Patrick Klint right now?"

"He's at Homey."

"Would you give Sergeant Stanton the vCard?"

"Yes, sir. Will there be anything else?"

"Please contact Patrick Klint and tell him to expect—"

"If you don't mind, Mr. Cummings," Heart said, "we'd prefer to not announce ourselves."

"As you wish. That's all, Lucy. Thank you."

"Yes, sir." The android left.

Heart turned around and watched her go. "She's quite — well, for lack a better word — fluid."

"Yes, SynthResearch is doing marvelous things with centralized cognizant linkages. An independent arti-brain is a long way off, but this is the next best thing."

"So we've seen. How far is Homey from here?"

Cummings tapped his hand-tab several times as the wall behind him transformed into a large map. "Metrofloat New York is on its southern drift. This puts us close, but I would estimate you have an hour's drive. Two, depending on your speed."

"You've been most helpful, Mr. Cummings."

***

They saw the complex long before landing. There were security protocols to follow and an ID verification process. Not just anybody could drive up for a look.

A woman greeted them, shielding her face with her hands. "You didn't pick the best time for a visit, Sergeant Stanton. We're about to get hit by a sandstorm." She stuck out a hand. "Sanora Babb, director."

She led them into the main building as the wind howled, and they all brushed the sand from their clothes. "I think it'll be a doozy," she said, leading them into an office. "I have to warn you. We're down to a skeleton crew and we've decided, considering the storm, to pull out. The shuttle is taking us back to Metrofloat New York, but we'll return tomorrow. By that time, the storm will have died down. It didn't seem worthwhile riding things out here. Working outside is difficult in a sandstorm, if not impossible."

"You have a Patrick Klint here?"

"Yes and no. He's here, but he's not part of my team. He came in a few months ago with a special security clearance from Head Office, setting himself up in a private shed on the far side of the compound. I have no contact with him whatsoever, although I was instructed to give him any help he wanted. However, he hasn't required any and never comes into the complex itself. On occasion, I've seen his flivver come and go, but that's it." She called up a map of the complex, standing in front of the display. "We're here, and his work shed is there. I haven't got much to help you in a sandstorm, but I can offer you goggles."

Five minutes later, they were trudging outside, leaning into the wind. Heart made the mistake of puffing air from his mouth and had to spit several times to rid himself of grains of sand. After about ten minutes, they arrived at the shed, only to discover the door was padlocked. They walked around the structure, peeking in windows, but found they had been blacked out. There was no sedan in sight.

"Now what?" Stanton yelled over the wind.

"We need to take a look inside."

"We don't have a warrant."

"You want to go back and get one?"

Heart grabbed hold of the padlock, examining it closely. He pulled, looked at the underside, and then put a finger on the touch pad. The light remained red.

"Let me try." Stanton seized the padlock and tugged several times. Then, with both hands, she held the padlock and pulled. The staple ripped out of the doorframe, and she dropped the lock on the ground. "It can't be this easy."

"I'm sure it isn't," Heart said.

She yanked open the door and they hurried inside before she pulled it shut. The force of the blown sand peppered the small building.

"See any lights?" he asked.

Feeling beside the door, Stanton touched a small panel. Lights came on across the shed, illuminating several workbenches. In one corner sat a bed beside an enclosed toilet, along with a refrigerator and a counter with a sink and microwave.

"Mr. Klint has made a self-sufficient life for himself out here in the desert," Heart said, stepping into the middle of the hut and looking around.

Stanton went over to one bench and studied the various tools lying about. "He has equipment to do just about anything."

"And what would that be?"

"Well, it doesn't look like he's doing research for WillMar."

She stopped in front of a cabinet beside another bench. Two hinged doors opened to either side from the middle. She pulled on the handle of the right side, revealing a series of drawers. In the middle one there was a mask or, rather, a face. She picked it up, holding it to the light. "Heart?"

"Yes?"

"Come look at this."

She turned back to the cabinet and opened another drawer.

Taking the face from her hand, he turned it over, examining both sides. "I don't recognize this face."

She held up another. "Recognize this?"

"That's the guy I met in the washroom."

Stanton put both faces back in their respective drawers and pulled out a third. "Oh, my."

"What?"

She held it up for him to see.

"Willard Bachmann. I wonder what else you're going to find in there."

Opening the left door, they checked each of the drawers, finding more faces, several sets of hands, and various ID chips.

"This guy has everything he needs to pass himself off as different people."

Combing the entire shed, they discovered equipment for disabling security, as well as for eavesdropping. There were also several weapons.

"This guy is prepared for war. I'd say there's no doubt about it: Patrick Klint is our guy." Heart turned a device, shaped somewhat like a pistol, over in his hand. "I have no idea what this is, but it makes me wonder if this wasn't how he fired that EMP at my autocab."

"We need an APB — armed and dangerous."

"Do it. We should get a team out here as soon as possible and tear this place apart. Who knows what we may have missed?"

"Call." She stood still, looking perplexed. "Call."

"What's the matter?"

"I'm not getting a signal. You try."

Heart touched his ear-tab. "Odd. I'm not getting anything either." He tapped the device. "System Check."

"It may be the storm."

"I'm not sure about that."

"What do you mean?"

"Judging by the look of this place," Heart said, glancing around, "it's well serviced. I can't believe a sandstorm would knock out all communications."

"We better get back to Metrofloat New York."

"Do you think we should be flying in this storm?"

"Do we have a choice?" Stanton asked. "We have a killer

running around, and judging by his available resources, he's far more dangerous than we believed."

The two officers put on their goggles, stepped out of the shed, and shut the door.

"Where's the lock?" Heart scanned the ground.

"I dropped it," she said, pointing. "Over there somewhere. I'm sure it's covered in sand."

The strength of the storm had substantially increased, and they spent fifteen minutes stumbling back to the main building. Sand had piled up against their flivver. After closing the doors against the strong winds, they brushed off both themselves and their seats.

"I'm going to find sand in my underwear." Heart blew spurts of air from between his lips, flicking grains from his mouth with a finger.

Stanton started the car and verified systems. "Everything is operational. I don't expect the storm to have any effect on our trip." The vehicle rose a few meters before turning ninety degrees. "We can keep trying communications. At some point we'll get away from whatever is causing the problem and we can report the APB."

There was a sudden flash of light to one side.

"What was that?" Stanton asked.

"Lightning."

"In a sandstorm?"

"Yup," Heart said. "I've been through a few of these over the years, and I've seen some spectacular displays. The settlements can have some exciting entertainment in the form of weather."

The waves of sand hitting the flivver were constant and loud. Two more flashes of lightning were followed by a rolling clap of thunder.

"Maybe it's going to take longer to get back," she said.

"I don't doubt it."

"We have headwinds, so we can't go as fast."

"Slow and steady," he said, glancing at the dashboard display and scanning the sky beyond the windows. "I can't see anything in any direction."

"It's bad. I've never driven through something like this."

A flash of light flew by the left side of the car.

Stanton jumped. "Did you see that?"

Heart twisted around in his seat to peer out the back window. "That wasn't a flash of lightning." There were clouds of sand everywhere and he strained to study the fuzzy scene behind them. As far as he could tell, there was nothing to see.

A blue flash suddenly arced out of the darkness and hit the rear of the car. There was a dull thud as the flivver shook. A buzzer sounded on the dashboard. He turned back to see Stanton scrolling through the various display options.

"We've lost thrusters." She touched several tab menus, scanning the data. "AG is functioning. We're not going down, but we can't go forward."

The flivver slowed and pivoted to the left. Howling winds raked the windows with sand as the vehicle began to tip and spin around.

"Whoa!" Heart braced himself. "We better land. We're being tossed around up here."

"Okay." Stanton touched a control and the screen showed a graphic display of their relationship to the ground. "We're close. I don't know how smooth this will be."

The bottom of the car touched something hard, bounced, and scraped along for several meters. An edge caught the ground and the entire vehicle tipped onto its right side. Heart fell against his door. Stanton put her hands up, bracing herself against the roof. For a moment, the vehicle remained suspended, and then it landed with a thump.

"We're down," she said.

"I wonder where."

"Out in the middle of nowhere."

"We can't see anything, but are you able to detect anything?"

She examined her display. "Radar shows flat land in all directions, but there is a small building two hundred and thirty-five meters to the right."

"It's got to be an overnighter."

"What's that?"

"Farmers get a fair distance off in the fields. Instead of going home they stay out for the night. An overnighter is a cabin with facilities, food, and a bed. We can ride things out there."

"We don't have any choice, do we?"

"Nope."

Heart put on his goggles and pointed to the right. "That way. Two hundred meters."

She put her goggles on as well. "And thirty-five."

They stepped into the blasting sand and headed off, side by side.

Chapter 12

Heart strained to shut the door against gusts of wind and sand. Stanton looked around the overnighter. "This is better than I thought."

"The company does provide some services to their workers. Though don't forget, it's all in the name of getting the most work out of them."

"I was picturing something more primitive."

The wind howled outside, making the small space cozier.

"Call." He tapped his ear-tab. "System Check."

"Still nothing? We're cut off."

"Or we're being jammed."

"Jammed?"

"It wasn't a lightning bolt that knocked out our thrusters."

"Okay. So what was it?"

"I saw the flash come from behind, not from above. I think our bad guy came back."

"You're kidding."

"I couldn't see the lock, could you? Yes, it could be buried by the sand, or our guy came back, saw we were there, and waited until the right moment to try and kill us."

"Why didn't he blast us? We couldn't move."

"I don't know. Was he disoriented by the sandstorm? Was he having problems, too?"

"I think you're wrong. I think it was a lightning bolt."

He shrugged. "Whatever the case, we'll be stuck here until the morning."

"I need to recharge."

"You mean eat?"

Stanton hesitated. "No, recharge."

"But you ate the other day."

"Yes, I can do it. I eat to take in nutrients for my brain. However, the rest of me is synthetic. It's a machine, so it needs power to run."

"Huh! How long can you go?"

"My power supply is good for a week. I like to exchange

supplies rather than recharge myself, because it's faster. Since we're out of touch and I don't have access to my backup supply, I should recharge myself."

"What about nutrients?"

"I have a nutritional supply pack, which is also good for a week. While I can eat, I don't have to take in much. A normal person eats to sustain their whole body. I only have to do it for my brain."

"Why don't you skip the hassle of food and just stick with your nutritional supply pack?"

"I could, but I don't want to." Stanton slumped into a folding chair. "I've given up just about everything else. I don't want to give it all up."

"But you do have to sleep?"

"Yes. My human brain has all the needs any other person would have. I have to sleep or I'd go crazy. It's my time to mentally recharge, both literally and figuratively."

Heart explored the refrigerator and freezer. "I see some frozen meals. Want to take a chance?"

"Sure."

"What do you want?"

"What do you have? That's the better question."

"Let's see." He pulled out boxes. "Mealworm stew. Fried locust. Cricket soup. Beetle stir-fry."

"I wonder how they taste reheated."

"It beats starving."

"How you whet my appetite! I'll try the locust. Even if it is reheated, I can't imagine how you can mess up that staple."

"We'll find out. For me, I'll have the stew. I love a good larva."

After microwaving their food, he joined her at the tiny table.

"There's only one bed," she said.

"There's a roll-out sleeping pad in that locker."

"Oh. Well, I can sleep sitting up."

"You can?"

"Yes. I can do a system lockdown to maintain position and

let my brain sleep, so I can sleep standing up if I have to."

"Is it uncomfortable?"

"I have the needs and wants I've always had, so I prefer sleeping in a prone position. It's more natural. It's part of our DNA. However, I'm not subject to the same restrictions as a human body and can do things the average person can't."

"Like sleeping sitting up."

"Yes."

"I take it you've had to make a lot of adjustments."

"That's an understatement! You're whole and have never had to experience using a prosth. It's not the same as a natural body part. It's an approximation. With an arti-hand you get tactile signals, but they aren't the same as what you feel with a real hand. You have to relearn basic motor skills because the signals the brain sends out to move an arm, for instance, are not the same for an arti-arm. It took months of physiotherapy to train myself to control my new body. Many times, I would reach out to grasp something and would either undershoot or overshoot my mark. It took practice to redevelop my hand–eye coordination." She held up her fork and chuckled. "I can't count the number of times I missed my mouth and stabbed myself in the face."

Heart smiled with her. "And now?"

"I've got used to it. It's become my new normal. I suppose everyone adjusts, but I didn't have a choice other than to accept." She glanced out the window. "Still, I miss my body."

He remained quiet, letting her talk.

"I miss feeling my muscles: moving, turning, running. I enjoyed getting into bed and stretching out between the sheets, extending my arms and legs, and experiencing that delicious connection with my body as I fell asleep." She looked at him. "I can still do that, but it doesn't feel the same as with a real body."

"But you're still you."

"Yes, but I don't always perceive it that way. I think I see myself how others see me. I mean... I see myself how I think others see me."

Heart pushed back in his chair, keeping one hand on the table. "How can we not be affected by the opinions of others?"

"I think I'm too sensitive."

He brushed his little finger against the back of her hand. "You need to hang around with a different group of people. People who are more accepting, more open. You find out humanity is not defined by a human hand or a human arm. It's something more. It's compassion, understanding, and love."

"Love?"

"I'm not thinking here of romantic love, but a love of life and a love of your fellow creatures."

"You're a poet."

"As you know, having your life upended forces you to rethink a lot of things. What's important? Who's important? What's valuable in life?"

"Any conclusions?" Stanton asked.

"Let's say the things I was striving for — career, money, position, and power — were taken away. Now I live with those who are struggling to get by, dealing with the inequities of life, and I think less about myself and more about others. Do I have problems? Yes, I do. But compared to the next guy, I'm the luckiest guy alive. I should complain? Ha!"

"We seem in agreement. That was my reason for wanting to be in the police force."

Heart picked up the empty food trays and tossed them in a trash compactor. He peeked out the window, studying the gusts of wind and sand.

"Is it dying down?" Stanton asked.

"Hard to tell."

"Let's try connecting. Call."

"Call. System Check."

"Still no go," she said. "How long are we going to be in this blackout?"

"I have no idea," he said, sitting back down.

They glanced at one another and then looked away. Heart tapped a finger on the tabletop. "Had sex yet?"

She looked at him, eyes wide. "What? No. I... well..."

He raised an eyebrow as she looked away. "I'm sorry. I'm getting too personal."

Stanton kept looking at the wall as she replied. "It's okay." She sighed. "I went to therapy."

Heart leaned back in his chair, crossing a leg over the other. "I'm sometimes overwhelmed by what happened, by how my life changed. Sure, I'm lucky. I know I've been given a unique opportunity. But I feel so much like an outsider now." She glanced at him. "I know it's my self-perception. Yes, I'm accepted at work. Yes, I'm accepted by my commander. Yes, I'm accepted by my colleagues — well, some of my colleagues, like yourself — but that's all on a business level. I have a difficult time imagining anything more personal."

"I know a woman who contracted necrofasc," Heart said. "She lost her right leg, midthigh. Then she lost her left leg below the knee. From what turned out to be negligence by the doctor, the necrofasc spread up the thigh and into her pelvis. Everything from her waist down is prosthetic. Gabrielle is a charming woman. I don't ever remember her being without suitors."

"Interesting story."

"We saw each other for a year."

"You did?"

"We had sex."

Her eyes widened. "What? How?"

"I'm certain you've, uh, explored yourself. Artificial body parts are different, but the technology today brings you functionality and appearance. Centuries ago, if you lost a leg, you ended up with something as primitive as a wooden peg strapped to your stump. Nowadays you have a functional leg that bends, twists, and acts like a human one. In fact, one could argue, when it comes to strength, agility, and speed, the arti-leg is better than the real thing. You have an enhanced body part, after all."

"But..."

"It's all functional, Elizabeth," Heart said. "You're still a woman. And I say that as a man speaking from experience. When you think about it, the current state of BCI is amazing. Science can connect all five senses to artificial ones. You can see, hear, touch, taste, and smell without natural organs. The first people I met when I came to the settlement were Sally and Christine. Christine is Sally's mother, but Christine was born a man. She's always felt like a woman, but she was given a man's body. The last time I saw her, she explained the arti-vag. When she transitions fully, she's going to get one. And when she does, she will complete the last step in medically becoming a fully functioning female."

"I'm not sure I can grasp what you're saying."

"What did your therapist say?" Heart asked.

"She's a nice lady, but she's dealing with theory. She has little or no experience with prosths, and she has no experience with synths. But you? You're talking the real thing."

"I think that's the biggest lesson I've learned while on the ground: acceptance. Short? Tall? Fat? Skinny? Whole? Prosths? It's the person who counts. As I said, you need to hang out with a different crowd. You'd be surprised how acceptance from others can go a long way to acceptance of yourself. Yes, we all must practice self-love, but it does the ego good to have somebody else show they accept us for who we are." He chuckled. "Now, I didn't say want us or love us or desire us. That's a whole other issue. But accept us? That's a good start."

"You paint a beautiful picture."

"Hey, I'll be the first to say life isn't always good. It has its challenges. But if we persist, we'll win."

"Are you always this nice?"

He smiled. "I have my moments, but I'm as flawed as the next guy. Don't think for a minute I'm perfect. On occasion I chew with my mouth open and belch." Heart rose and walked to the sanitary cubicle. "You insist on sitting?"

"Yes, it's only one night." Once alone, Stanton hiked up her shirt, opened a slot in her waist, and pulled out a small rectangular object. She positioned the Wi-Fi charger on a magnetic wall connector.

Heart returned and put his ear-tab on the bedside table. "I'm setting my proximity detector for two kilometers, just in case our bad guy decides to show up."

He turned off the lights, stripped down to his underwear, pulled a blanket over himself, and glanced over at the table. Stanton sat motionless in the semi-darkness, eyes shut. The wind outside had died down. It still blew in gusts, but it sounded as if the worst was over. Heart was sure they'd be able to call for help in the morning.

***

It was quiet. There was no wind, no sound of driving sand. Did he have to pee? Turning his head, Heart looked at Stanton. She remained unchanged from when he'd fallen asleep. Pulling back the blanket, he sat on the edge of the bed. There was a distorted square of light on the floor; the moon was out. He got up to use the cubicle.

Finished, Heart went to the window and stared out at the moonlit fields. The stars were out and the Milky Way was visible. All was calm and peaceful. He stared up at the sky and located Orion. He saw the box formed by the stars and counted out those in the middle: one, two, and three.

His ear-tab beeped from the table so he put it on. "Analyze."

A light was moving across the sky. A long-distance transport? Was it getting closer?

Heart touched his partner's shoulder. "Stanton?" He nudged her arm. "Stanton?"

"Yes?" She took her charger from the wall and put it back in her side.

"I think we have company." He rushed back to the bed and dressed hurriedly.

She stood by the window. "My telescopic sight is showing a flivver. But even with night-vision enhancement, I can't yet tell the number of passengers."

"I bet it's one. That's all he needs."

"Who?"

"Patrick Klint. I'm certain he's come back to finish what he started." Heart buttoned his shirt, got flustered by a mismatch, and had to redo them. "Are you ready?"

"For?"

"We're exiting, ASAP. Once he sees this overnighter so close to our flivver, I have no doubt he'll be dropping in for a visit. And I'm sure it won't be friendly." He moved to the door. "Ready?"

"Yes."

"Let's go." Heart pulled open the door and let his partner pass before pulling it shut. They darted behind the hut toward a dry irrigation channel. "Let's hide in there and then move away." They scurried along the cement bottom for twenty meters and then stopped and peeked over the side. Heart touched his ear-tab for the display and whispered. "Night vision."

They watched as a darkened flivver glided to the ground, landing not far from theirs. All the running lights had been turned off. As they watched, the right door opened and a man emerged. He reached back into the vehicle, pulling out something long and thin. Patrick Klint took several steps toward the overnighter and hoisted a launcher onto his right shoulder. Gripping the weapon with one hand, he used the other to adjust something on the top. He took a forward stance, pointing the firearm at the cabin. With a bang, a flame spurted from the back as the front erupted and rocket exhaust shot toward the overnighter. An explosion followed, and the cabin disintegrated in a ball of fire.

Klint fiddled again with some settings, turned, and pointed the weapon at their flivver. Another detonation destroyed the flivver. He walked back to his car and put the launcher away. When he stood up, their night vision revealed he now carried a gun in his right hand. He walked by their burning flivver and strode toward the remains of the overnighter.

Heart touched Stanton's arm and whispered, "Let's go." They climbed out of the channel and headed toward Klint's car. They kept glancing his way as they scurried across the open plain. Klint strolled around the remains of the cabin, stopping to move something with his foot.

Stealthily, the two officers got into the flivver, Heart in the driver's seat.

"What makes you think he doesn't have fingerprint ignition enabled?" Stanton stooped over the open door.

"I have no idea but I'm hoping, as a company car, it doesn't." He pressed the dash-tab several times. "Damn." He looked through the windshield at Klint, his outline visible by the fire.

"Let me try."

Heart and Stanton climbed over one another. "MetPol override security clearance authorization Alfa Alfa three-zero-five." She touched the screen and the display lit up.

Klint again kicked something before backing up several paces. He stood looking at the fire when he suddenly spun around. He dashed toward them.

"Go! He's seen us," Heart said.

Stanton poked the display and seized the steering wheel. The flivver rose as she pulled back, and they both heard several sharp pings.

Twisting the wheel, she slammed her foot on the accelerator. The flivver banked in a steep climb and the pinging stopped.

"Let's try communication," Stanton said. "Call."

"Call. System Check."

"Nothing."

"I find that hard to believe," Heart said. "Has Klint somehow jammed the area? Or has he locked us out of the network?"

"I don't know."

"Where are we?"

Stanton brought up a map. "We're about twenty klicks from Homey."

"We didn't get far in the storm. However, this means Klint has a good hike back. That will keep him out of trouble for a while."

"What should we do?"

"We need help, and we need it fast." He pointed to the map. "Farm Settlement Thirty-Five is straight north, eighty-five kilometers. Let's see if we can get help in solving our communications problem."

"Okay," she said. "The storm has passed and the air's calm. Let's see how much I can get out of this thing. It doesn't have the power of the squad car."

Twenty minutes later, the lights of a town came into view. "I'm still not getting anything. I'm going straight to the local precinct." She called up a map and located the local constabulary. Sending the coordinates to the autopilot, she took her hands off the wheel. In ten minutes the car had glided over a building, done a slow turn, and settled into the parking lot in front of the main entrance. They bolted into the police station.

Heart leaned against the main counter, puffing from the exertion. "We need help."

The officer sat behind a security window, staring at a display showing a movie. "What's the nature of the problem?"

"My name is Detective Heart, and this is—"

The man looked up, alarmed. "You're Detective Heart?"

"Yes, and this is Sergeant Stanton."

The man reached under the counter, ducking out of sight. A steel protection plate slammed down over the window. At the same time, a cage barrier slid across the front door, sealing the reception area. An alarm sounded, and a red light on a wall began to flash. Four vents in the ceiling expelled clouds of gas.

Heart pounded on the protection plate. "Wait. What the hell are you doing? Stop! Stop!" He sensed himself going under and the last thing he saw was the floor coming up to meet him.

***

"How long?"

Stanton sat on the edge of a metal bench fixed to the wall.

"Twenty minutes, I'd say."

"How about you?"

"I didn't go under."

"You didn't?"

"No."

"Why not?"

"I shut my air intake as soon as I saw the gas and switched to reserve oxygen. I'm good for an hour."

Heart propped himself up on one elbow. "Why did they do that?"

"You and I have a notorious reputation."

"Pardon?"

"Half a dozen officers burst in, brandishing weapons. I thought it best they didn't know I was a synth, so I pretended to be knocked out by the gas like you. I overheard them talking about us. Patrick Klint is innovative and, as you said, skillful. They can't verify our identities because our IDs are not in the system. Klint must have removed us. We couldn't communicate, not because we were being jammed but because the system wouldn't link to unknown IDs. On top of it all, Klint posted official bulletins on the settlement police network declaring us public enemies, wanted on numerous crimes, and with the warning that we were armed and dangerous. We're lucky they didn't shoot us on sight."

Heart sat up, swinging his feet over the side of the bench. He put his hands on his knees and glanced around the jail cell. "They certainly took that bulletin to heart."

"I can't blame them for being cautious. I'd do the same thing," she said.

"So, what's happening right now?"

"I assume they're waiting for us to wake up so we can be interrogated."

"What are we going to do? Every minute we stay here is another minute Patrick Klint is out there, plotting God knows what." He massaged his temples.

"We need to contact Headquarters."

"Voynich?"

"They took everything from us, including the communicator."

"Then we need to get it back." He shook his head to clear it.

"I have a plan: let's bust out."

"You have a secret stash of plastic explosives?"

"Better." Stanton went to the cell door. "MetPol override security clearance, authorization Alfa Alfa three-zero-five." She pushed on the door. It didn't budge.

"Nice try."

She knelt to examine the lock. "Interesting."

"Why?"

"This is an older model. I guess upgrades in the settlements take longer."

"Life in the settlements can be backward. We're the last to get any improvements."

"MetPol override security clearance, authorization Kilo Alfa four-six-zero-one-seven-zero-four." She pushed the door, and this time it swung open.

"Whoa!" Heart jumped up. "Neat trick."

"They took my ear-tab without realizing I also have all functionality built in."

"Let's not tell them."

"We're going to have to act fast. Somebody's probably watching us, so we don't have much time."

They stepped into the hall and closed the cell door.

"We need to get that communicator." Stanton sprinted to the end of the hall and ran a finger over the lock. She repeated the code and opened the door. A siren sounded as an overhead beacon flashed red.

"Shit," Heart said.

She rattled off the code once again once they had both slipped through. "Seal all doors."

They ran down the hall. Passing an entrance identified as Squad Room, they heard yelling from inside. Somebody yanked several times on the handle, kicking the door when it wouldn't open.

Reaching the end of the hallway, they found two doors: one marked Reception and one Front Office.

"As soon as I unseal the door, I want you to get in there and disable whoever's manning the desk." Stanton knelt by the door and touched a keypad. A wall panel opened and she put her hand inside the box. "Ready?"

"Do it."

She pressed a button, recited the clearance code, and said, "Unseal."

Heart shoved the office door open and burst into the room. The wireless stun gun hit him square in the chest. There was a crackling sound and he remained fixed on the spot, his body convulsing. The noise stopped abruptly, and he collapsed to the floor.

Stanton marched into the room, heading for the officer at the desk. He stared at her, surprised, and swung the gun from Heart to her and fired. The blue flash of the electrical discharge crackled across the room. She didn't stop. Perplexed, the officer fired again and again. Stanton strode up to him and ripped the weapon out of his hand. Grabbing him by the front of his uniform with one hand, she lifted him off the ground. He gasped as his feet kicked the air. She pulled his service pistol out of its holster and tossed it aside and then unclipped a pair of handcuffs from his belt. Slamming him into his desk chair, she cuffed one of his hands as he stared at her, slack-jawed. She dragged him to the wall, wrapped chain around a pipe, and secured his other hand. "Don't move," she said.

Stanton hurried to her partner and crouched down. "Heart! Heart!" He groaned as she supported his head. "My God, are you all right?"

"Holy crap, did that ever hurt!" His eyes rolled around.

"Can you get up?"

"Call me in an hour. I like the floor."

"Let me find our stuff. We need to get the hell out of here."

She rushed to the officer's desk, opening every drawer but finding nothing. Looking around, she spied two cabinets separated by a small table. There, on a corner of the table, lay their confiscated items. She applied her ear-tab and holstered her gun.

Stanton picked up the remaining articles and returned to Heart. She knelt, put his ear-tab in place, placed his gun back in its shoulder holster, and shoved the communicator into one of his pockets.

He grunted.

"Let's go, Detective." Slipping one hand under his arm, she grabbed Heart's forearm with the other and hauled him into a standing position.

"Not good. Feeling wobbly."

"Walk, damn it!"

Heart took two steps and buckled, but she managed to catch him.

"Oh, for crying out loud!" Stanton got him standing again, bent down, and threw him over her shoulder. She walked out of the front office to reception and said the code. "Unseal." Crossing reception, she repeated the authorization and walked out the front door. Klint's car remained parked off to one side.

Once Heart was seated, she took over the controls. The car rose over the two-story precinct just as two pings sounded against the underside of the flivver. She glanced back to see a squad car at the building's entrance. A cop stood by the driver's side, aiming straight at them.

Banking over the roof, Stanton raced out of town toward the shadowy, open fields. She shook Heart by the arm. "Okay, nap time's over. Back to work."

"What?" His head bobbed around. "Mommy?"

"Cut it out. Try to contact Voynich."

Heart patted down his clothes and pulled out the communicator, fiddling with the device. "No go. Nothing." He tried his ear-tab. "We're still cut off."

"What do we do? Where do we go?"

"Head for FS45. I've got friends."

Chapter 13

Sipping Yerba, Heart had just finished explaining to Wang what had happened to him and Stanton.

"Mealworm stew, Sergeant?" Wang asked, placing one mechanical arm on the countertop for balance as he filled her gourd.

"Sure."

Looking thoughtful, Wang wandered down the counter to other customers.

Stanton leaned over to Heart, whispering, "Should you be telling him all the details of a police investigation?"

"I trust Wang with my life."

She shrugged. "Okay."

"Wang fixes things. He'll fix this."

"So he's a miracle guy with connections?"

"Something like that."

Wang ambled back, setting two plates in front of the officers. "Eat. Give me the communicator, Heart." He disappeared around the corner without another word.

Stanton examined her stew appreciatively and picked up a slice of flatbread. "This is rather civilized."

"Not what you expected out here, is it?" Heart poked at larvae.

"Sorry," she said. "That came out the wrong way."

"No apology necessary. I've come to understand floaters have a distorted view of the ground, but the people here are like everybody else. They just don't have the same resources and opportunities as you have in the city."

"I should be more accepting."

"We all have biases. You grow up in the city, you think like the city — whether you know it or not."

Wang came back and set the communicator down, his face grave. "There's an APB out for both of you."

Heart rolled his eyes.

"All the settlements have been alerted to treat you as armed and dangerous. You two are in big trouble."

Heart picked up the device.

"It took a little fiddling, but I got it to work. Despite the eighty-one ninety-two-bit certificate, I was able to determine this device has a unique ID connected to Voynich, which your man blocked. I modified the ID."

"Should I ask how?"

Wang picked up their plates without comment and walked over to the sink.

Heart pressed Call. There was a buzz and then silence. This sequence repeated itself, and after the third buzz there was a noise followed by a thump. A distant voice said, "Damn." A few more indistinct noises were followed by a clear signal. "Voynich."

"Good morning, sir. Did I wake you?"

"Heart?"

"Yes, sir."

"Is this Heart, the criminal extraordinaire and mastermind of dastardly deeds?"

"My reputation precedes me."

"Your Patrick Klint has done interesting things with our computer systems. You two are unwelcome just about everywhere. Heck, I doubt the Mars colonies would have you."

"I hope you can rectify that and as quickly as possible. We stopped at the Farm Settlement Thirty-Five precinct, and they were not friendly. In fact, they put us behind bars."

"I'm not surprised. Robbery, extortion, murder — the list goes on and on. I bet you take candy from babies."

"Since we busted out—"

"What?" Voynich guffawed. "You broke out of jail? I know Chief Fife. I'm sure he'll be none too pleased with you making a fool out of his people. Where are you now?"

"Farm Settlement Forty-Five. How soon could you get us reactivated?"

"I've had my team on it since we first found out early this morning. You're both now back online, but stay put. I'm afraid well-meaning law enforcement that are not yet privy to the news of your exoneration might overzealously shoot first and ask questions later. I'll contact FS45 right away and assure them the APB is a mistake and both of you are fine, upstanding citizens."

"Thank you, sir."

"Voynich out."

Heart placed the communicator back in the pocket of his jacket.

"Now what?" Stanton asked.

"We wait."

"That doesn't seem productive."

He shrugged. "Until Voynich clears us, there doesn't seem much else to do."

She put her elbows on the counter and slumped over in defeat. "Humph."

"Wang?" Heart beckoned him over. "What do I owe you?"

"Let's see. Three Yerbas. Two stews. Four pieces of flatbread. That works out to one hundred and eighteen credits."

Heart gaped at his friend.

"I can take my ID back," Wang said, almost snarling. "Besides, don't you big-city cops have expense accounts?"

Heart shut his mouth and rolled his eyes. "Okay, I'm forever grateful," he said, tapping the POS.

"As you should be." With that, Wang walked away to serve his other customers.

"So, we wait," Stanton said.

"If you don't mind, I'd like a shower and a change of clothes."

***

As Heart and Stanton neared the Low Cost Lodge, Sally hobbled out the front door, waving her arms.

"Matty! Matty!" Her face was contorted in anguish.

"What's the matter?"

"Come quick! Mom's been hurt."

"What?"

Not waiting for an explanation, they dove up the stairs and hurried down the hall. Christine sat crying at the kitchen table, her face in her hands.

"Christine, my God, what's wrong?" Heart crouched down in front of her. She sniffed as he edged her hand away from her face. A small trace of blood came from the corner of her mouth.

"Who did this?"

"It's nothing." Christine turned her head away, covering her mouth with her hand.

"Who did this?" he repeated, examining her face and moving her chin to look at it from a different angle. "Explain to me what happened."

"The" — she sniffed — "the city representative of the farming company showed up this morning."

"Yes."

"He wasn't pleased about the latest production quotas."

"Nothing new there."

"He wanted to skip a week's pay to punish everybody. I protested. I tried to explain how people live day to day and how losing a week's pay would break them."

Heart just managed to control his growing anger. "Go on."

She blew her nose. "He got angry."

"And?"

"He slapped me." Heart gently touched her cheek as she spoke. "He drew blood. I think he was wearing a ring."

"I've always regretted not standing up for you that first time."

"Matty—"

"I said I would never let that happen again."

"Matty—"

"I've got something to do."

"Please don't. It's nothing. I don't want any trouble."

Heart held Christine's hands. "I don't ask for politeness and respect. I demand it. Believe me, I'm not going to sit idly by when somebody violates the rules of common human decency. That's unforgivable."

Heart stood up and turned to Stanton. "I have to go to the farmers' union."

"What are you going to do?"

"Something I should have done a long time ago."

Without another word, Heart left and purposefully hiked the four blocks to the union building. Stanton trailed.

"You're angry," she said.

"Yes."

"Are you going to do something you'll regret?"

"Maybe. But this is something I have to do."

Heart pressed a thumb to the lock at the main door. Gaining entrance, they walked to the back office.

"Where is he?" Heart demanded.

Cesar looked up from his desk. "Uh-oh."

"Where's the city rep, Cesar?"

"Listen, Matt—"

"Right now. And it's Detective Heart. This is about a charge of assault and battery."

"Oh boy."

"Cesar, come on. I can't let this little shit get away with what he's done."

"But it's personal with you and Christine."

"Damn right it is!"

Cesar pushed back in his chair and sighed. "Albert Anastasia. He's second to your old friend."

Heart paced up and down the length of the small office.

"To who?" Stanton asked.

"Charlie Vance," Cesar said. "They go way back."

"Yes, Heart told me the story."

Heart stopped short. "Where is Anastasia now?"

"He's got a security detail."

"How many?"

"Four."

"Where?"

Cesar sighed. "Ernie's."

Heart frowned. "Ernie's? Why?"

"He said he wanted to have lunch and check out some local

color."

"Oh, he's slumming it. That pretentious little prick."

Cesar stood. "Listen, Matt—"

"No, that's it." Turning on his heel, Heart said over his shoulder, "My mind's made up."

Exiting the office, he tramped back down the street. Stanton and Cesar followed, apprehensive.

Stanton glanced up at the scorching sun. "How hot does it get here?"

"I've seen it get over fifty," Heart said. "If you can afford it you can buy a cooljack."

She looked down at the puffs of dust rising with Heart's every step.

Two blocks down, they came to a two-story warehouse. In front was a large sign with Ernie's Entertainment Emporium written in animated, colorful letters. Underneath, messages scrolled by: Best insects in town. Come for the food, stay for the fun. Meet new friends.

Twin doors slid open as they approached, and a blast of cool air rushed out. They entered to subdued lighting and the din of voices and music coming from the back. An out-of-tune voice struggled to sing the latest pop song. Off to one side, several people sat in front of gambling machines. Bright lights blinked, bells rang, and whistles sounded.

A woman came up to Heart, putting a mechanical arm around his shoulders. "Matthew, you've come back to me."

"Hi, Jessica. Where's the floater?"

"Beats me. I've been upstairs with a client." She kissed his cheek. "I'm free right now."

Heart put his arm around her waist and squeezed. "This is business," he said.

"Go see Ernie. He's up at the bar," she said.

"Thanks."

Heart wound his way between tables, mostly occupied by men. Stanton and Cesar followed. Stanton glanced back curiously at Jessica as she climbed onto a low platform and began gyrating before three men.

"Why are all these people here? Shouldn't they be working?" Stanton asked.

"They all work on rotating shifts," Cesar said. "Any day of the week could be the weekend for some workers. Ernie's is busy all the time."

They had come to a long counter with a slanted mirror suspended above. A woman glided down the length of the bar to greet them. From the waist down, her body was nothing more than a mechanized cart on four wheels. "Matthew, good to see you! Are you going to give us a tune?" She leaned over the bar and kissed him on the cheek.

"Not today, Gabrielle," Heart said. "I'm here on business. May I speak to Ernie?"

"Sure. I'll get him. He's out back doing stock."

The woman rolled away, disappearing through a door.

Stanton stared after her. "Is that the one you...?"

"Yes," Heart said. "She's married to Ernie."

On the stage, a young man with a prosthetic arm and leg held a microphone to his mouth, tilting his head back to wail along with the lyrics scrolling by on a screen behind him. People from several tables at the front yelled encouragement, despite his inability to carry a tune.

"Matt."

They all turned back to see a muscular man with a mechanical left arm.

"Hey, Ernie," Heart said. "I see you got your arti-flesh."

"Just the right one. The left's supposed to come in next week." Ernie held out his arm. "Feel that."

Heart touched the forearm and grabbed at the flesh. "Good quality."

Proud, Ernie held his arm up and flexed. "Impressive, yes?"

"Ernie, I'm here on business."

"Uh-oh." Ernie rubbed his forehead. "I should have known you wouldn't be here in the middle of the day to sing us a song."

"Where are the floaters?"

Ernie smiled. "How about a free drink for you and your

friends?"

"Ernie..." Heart pursed his lips.

"Okay, okay. The five of them have a secluded dance table underneath the private rooms." He pointed in the general direction.

At the far side of the building, on the second floor, were a series of rooms that could be accessed by a walkway overlooking the bar. A woman, all her limbs mechanical, led a man with artificial arms to a room halfway down and they disappeared inside.

"Where?"

"See the side exit?"

"Yes."

"Just to the left."

"Okay." Heart stepped away.

"Matt?"

He stopped. "Yes?"

Ernie shook a finger. "Take it outside, understand?"

"I will."

Heart and company crossed the room, passing through a small archway and into an alcove. Five men sat at a semi-circular table in front of a raised platform. A woman with arti-flesh arms, dressed in a skimpy outfit, pranced back and forth while a waiter placed plates of food in front of each patron.

"Albert Anastasia?" Heart planted himself behind the man sitting in the middle. Guards on either side rose from the table and stood in front of Heart.

"Who wants to know?" the one on the left asked.

"Detective Matthew Heart of the Metropolitan Police."

The remaining men stood and the two guards parted. The man in the middle came forward and smiled. "My name is Albert Anastasia. Pleased to meet you, Detective—"

Heart slapped him.

All four security men took a step forward but stopped when Anastasia raised his hand. "I could have your badge, Detective," he said, rubbing his cheek.

The dancer hurried from the platform and disappeared.

"What to think of a man who strikes a woman?" Heart asked, disgusted.

"Ah, so you're here to defend the honor of Mx. Elbe."

"The charge is assault and battery."

"Witnesses?"

Heart gritted his teeth as Anastasia turned to the guards. "Did anybody see someone strike Mx. Elbe?" They all shook their heads and he turned back to Heart with a shrug.

"Do I take you in?" Heart countered.

"You won't get anything to stick." He eyed Heart. "How about an alternative? Man to man? I owe you for the slap."

One of the guards said, "You show him, boss."

Anastasia smirked.

"Outside," Heart said, stepping out of the way.

"By all means," Anastasia replied.

They withdrew from the alcove and headed toward the side entrance. Their presence stirred those in the building and somebody yelled, "Fight!" The music sputtered out, and the sound of chairs scraping the floor replaced it as people stampeded for the exit.

Anastasia sauntered out to the middle of a wide laneway and wheeled around. His guards took up position behind him as other patrons flowed out and formed a circle around Heart and Anastasia.

"So, Detective," Anastasia said. "First one down, winner take all?"

Heart took off his jacket and held it out to Stanton. "Take this."

She rolled her eyes as she did so.

Heart looked up at the blazing sun. Already he could feel a bead of sweat trickle down his back. He and Anastasia stared each other down as the four guards spaced themselves out, scoffing.

"Mr. Anastasia is a three-time karate champion with a seventh-degree Dan rank," said the one on the right. "Good luck. You're going need it."

A general murmur rose from the crowd. "What's going

on?" someone asked, to which another replied, "Floater. MetPol."

A woman yelled, "You can take him, Heart!"

A faint buzz sounded and Stanton reached into Heart's jacket pocket, retrieving the communicator.

Heart and Anastasia were moving in circles, facing one another. Each held up their fists, their gazes darting from face to hands and back again in assessment. All eyes were intent on the fighters.

"Heart?" Stanton said.

Anastasia threw a punch and Heart ducked.

"Heart?"

Anastasia kicked, but Heart blocked the move. They bounced back and forth, each focused solely on his opponent.

"Heart!"

Heart turned and barked, "What do you want?"

There was a crackle of electricity and a faint cry from behind. Heart jerked back to see Anastasia fall to the ground, moaning. The crowd gasped.

Heart threw up his arms. "What the hell did you do that for?"

Stanton holstered her gun. "You dropped your guard. He was going to hit you."

"What? You distracted me!" He stood, hands on hips, and huffed.

The disconcerted guards gaped stupidly at their prone boss.

Stanton handed Heart his jacket. "Let's go. Voynich called and wants us back right away."

Just then a guard stepped forward. "You bitch!" He threw a punch at Stanton.

She seized his fist in midair and held fast. The guard glared at her, but his expression turned to one of surprise. "Ow. Ow! OW!" He looked pained as he dropped to his knees.

Stanton released him and he huddled on the ground, holding his hand. "Shit!"

A second guard rushed her and threw a punch, but she blocked it easily. He followed with a hook, which she also blocked. Stanton slapped him and he stumbled back, stunned. Grabbing him by the underarm and leg, she hoisted him over her head and tossed him at the other two guards, causing them all to tumble to the ground. They stared back in disbelief.

The crowd inched back, murmuring. "Whoa!"

"Pick up your boss and get out of here." She pointed at the guards. "Now! Before I really get pissed."

Stanton took Heart by the elbow, steering him to the street. The crowd parted to let them pass.

"Voynich has restored our IDs," she said. "All false bulletins have been retracted and notifications sent to all precincts. We're in the clear."

"I could have beat him," Heart said.

"I'm sure you could have. But Voynich wants us back ASAP, and I couldn't wait for you two to finish dancing."

"Aw, jeez."

Stanton patted him on the shoulder. "Next time."

Chapter 14

Voynich sat, half turned toward the window of his office. "When we first met, I talked to you about the balance in our lives — between order on one side and chaos on the other. I mentioned how a little greed is good, but too much greed can threaten that balance. From everything you've told me, someone wants to upset that balance. Someone has gotten greedy and isn't satisfied with the status quo but wants everything." He swung back toward Stanton and Heart. "I admit it. I like the way my life is, and I don't want to lose it. I'll be damned if I'm going to let somebody else's idea of right and wrong jeopardize everything I've built. We need to find this guy, and we need to stop him."

"Face, fingerprints, ID," Heart said. "This guy has cornered the market on everything necessary to turn himself into somebody else. Who do we look for?"

Stanton nodded in agreement.

"Where did this start?" Voynich asked. "Who would know?"

"I'd still like to interview Marie Amble again," Heart said, "even if we have to haul her in and intimidate her into talking. Who cares about her lawyer? She's hiding something."

"SynthResearch?"

"Delambre was also hiding something. But he's dead."

"Eden? A colleague?"

"My impression is that Eden's a good guy and is unaware of what's going on. Maybe a colleague of Delambre knows something, but I'm sure he was overly cautious. The best way to keep a secret is to not tell anybody, and he probably wasn't sharing his secrets at work."

"Did Delambre and Amble know one another?" Voynich asked.

"I would have said no, but now that you're asking, I have to say I don't know. We need to investigate a possible connection."

"The team reported in from Homey ten minutes ago."

"And?"

"Your man has disappeared. The shed was cleaned out. Forensics is going over everything, but the preliminary report states there is no human DNA. That corresponds with Stanton's assessment."

"We took his car," Heart said.

"There were several vehicles parked at the facility. I've set up checkpoints at every city portal to examine all incoming vehicles: cars, trucks, cruisers, skytrains — anything. We don't know what we're looking for. Besides, there are other, unauthorized, points of entry. I'm always surprised at how inventive people are when it comes to circumventing the law. No matter how tight we think we've got things, somebody comes along and discovers a loophole we never thought of. It makes me shake my head and chuckle."

"We'll start with Marie Amble and then go back to SynthResearch."

"Let's stay in close contact. I'll let you know if anything turns up at the portals. If you think of anything, no matter how insignificant, let's discuss. I'm sure we're missing something important, and our man is going to slip in undetected."

***

Stanton and Heart stood at the door of Amble's penthouse. There was no answer.

"Now what?" Heart said.

"May I help you?"

They turned to look at the door-tab. A man's face on the display stared back.

"Who are you?"

"I'm the building super, Gregory. Ms. Amble is not in."

"Detective Heart and Sergeant Stanton of MetPol. Do you know when Ms. Amble will be back?"

"She's gone over to the park for her morning walk."

"Any particular path?"

"She likes to walk around the reservoir."

Within a few minutes, they found themselves at the artificial lake, speculating on Amble's route.

"You go left, and I'll go right. One of us will run into her." Heart touched his ear-tab. "Stay in touch."

After ten minutes, he came across a couple with their backs toward him, standing by the water. As he got closer, he realized they were arguing. The man seized the woman's arm and pulled her close. She pounded her free hand on his chest. "Stop it! Stop it! You're crazy!" He slapped her and she staggered back, falling to the ground.

Heart saw the woman's face. It was Marie Amble. "Hey!" He ran up. "Are you all right?" Two hands seized him by the shoulders, and the next moment he was airborne. He hit the surface of the reservoir with a loud splash, his mouth filling with murky water. He thrashed about before managing to right himself. "Goddammit!" He spat several times, wiping his face as he touched his ear-tab and waded through the thigh-deep water back to shore. "Stanton, help! Our guy is assaulting Amble."

The assailant had lifted Amble off the ground and had her pushed up against a tree. His hand was around her throat. "I will stop you," he said, raising his fist for another strike.

Heart ran up and seized the raised arm. "Stop! Stop!"

The man flung him aside and raised his fist again. Heart fired. The bullet grazed the upper arm, tearing fabric and leaving a visible gouge in the biceps. The man paused, but as Heart watched, the gouge filled in and sealed itself up. Heart kept his gun trained on the assailant. "Okay, big guy. Let's take this nice and slow."

Letting Amble drop, the man turned and stepped toward Heart. The officer fired a bullet into the synth's shoulder. His body jerked, yet he continued forward. Heart fired again. Seizing Heart's gun hand by the wrist, the assailant pointed it away. Heart struggled but couldn't break free of the grip, so he grabbed the gun with his left hand and stuck the barrel against the attacker's forearm. "Explosive." He fired.

There was a loud pop and Heart tumbled to the ground.

The man stared, uncomprehending, at the stump of his arm, which was crackling with flying sparks. He bolted and disappeared into the park.

Heart set down his gun and pried the fingers of the severed hand from his wrist. He struggled with the thumb, but it finally gave way and the hand dropped off. "Shit!" Heart scooped up his firearm, recoiling from the severed appendage. As he holstered his weapon, he looked over at Amble. "Are you all right?"

She sat at the base of the tree trunk, scared and disoriented. "He's crazy. He was going to kill me."

At the sound of rapid steps, Heart turned to see Stanton running up to them.

"You missed all the fun," Heart said.

Stanton knelt and picked up the severed hand. "So I see."

Heart turned back to Amble. "No hiding anything, Ms. Amble. Give me the truth. Who was that man?"

"That was Willard Bachmann."

***

The three collected themselves on a park bench.

"Bachmann is dead," Stanton said, studying the woman's reaction. "We saw his body. Forensics examined it and verified the fingerprints, the DNA, and the personal ID chip."

"Yes, I know." Amble sobbed intermittently, blowing her nose. "That's what makes this all the more heartbreaking."

"What do you mean?"

"It's him, but it's not him." Her voice cracked. "I didn't want to lose him but he became so different, so distant. He went crazy at times and I had to let him go. I couldn't stand it any longer."

Stanton looked at Heart and shrugged, unable to comprehend what Amble meant.

"Ms. Amble," Heart said, "what do you mean when you say that man is Willard Bachmann? That man is a synth."

"Technically, he's an android."

"So, there's no human brain in there?"

"No."

"So, what is in there?"

"An arti-brain."

"But that's impossible. We've seen androids with arti-brains and they can't behave like that man does," Heart said.

"That's true, but the professor—"

"Professor Delambre?"

"Yes. He was working on extending BCIs and memory reconstruction."

"For what purpose?"

"Even though nobody's ever replicated the functionality of the human brain, they've come up with fancy algorithms to fake being human. Nobody's ever matched it. The professor thought to tackle the problem from a different angle. If he couldn't recreate the human thought process in an arti-brain, why not transfer the thought process from a human being into an arti-brain?"

"Okay," Heart said.

"Willard became sick."

"We found that much out."

"All of his money, all of his power, couldn't help. He was doomed."

"Dr. McGaugh said he was in remission."

"Maybe so, but it was all experimental and nothing was guaranteed." Amble wiped her nose again. "But that wasn't the problem. The disease had already taken its toll. Willard knew his faculties were diminished, that he wasn't the man he once was. Remission wasn't his goal — he wanted to get back what he'd lost. He became obsessed with Delambre's experiment, talking the professor into transferring his thoughts into an arti-brain."

"What happened?"

"Something went wrong. The resulting brain wasn't like Willard. It was different, strange. It had Willard's memories and his abilities, but it didn't think like him. Like Willard, it was angry and ambitious, but it was also violent and single-mindedly ruthless. It wasn't in command — it was controlling and cruel. Whatever was wrong with Willard became amplified."

"And what happened to you two?"

"I became scared of him — both the human and the android. I asked him to go away because I couldn't deal with what he'd become."

"Then why did you hide the android from us when we visited you?"

"He said he would kill me if I said anything," Amble said.

"Why did he meet you here in the park?"

"He knew about my walks, and he wanted to tell me he loved me. It was the old Willard talking, but I told him he needed help. I said I didn't want him like this. He got angry and, if you hadn't stepped in, I'm convinced he would have killed me like he killed Delambre."

"You know, then," Heart said.

"He told me."

"What do you think he's planning on doing next?"

"When he talks..." She shook her head, eyes downcast. "I don't know. It's muddled, confused. He doesn't always make sense. Like the real Willard, I think the android is exhibiting signs of dementia, but unlike him, there's no physical side to the ailment. It's a malfunctioning thought process in the arti-brain that's leading to bizarre and unpredictable behavior."

"Did he indicate if he's planning anything specific?"

"I don't know. All along he's rambled on about wanting to take over. Has his faulty mind distorted this ambition to take over the OligCouncil into a perverted plan to get rid of everybody? Willard was competitive in business. Has that been amplified into a ruthless combativeness?"

"Where is he likely to go now?"

"I don't know. Keep in mind that thing has Willard's knowledge. He knows Willard's secrets, his passcodes, and everything necessary to gain access to his companies. Don't forget Willard headed up one of the largest military manufacturers."

Heart looked at Stanton and shook his head. "I think we're in trouble."

"But what type of trouble?"

"Not knowing makes it worse. Right now, I'm not sure where to start."

"Ms. Amble," Stanton said, "we'd like to put you in protective custody."

"Now?"

"It's for your own good."

"Where?"

"An undisclosed location we'll have to work out. We'll take you back to your penthouse so you can prepare a bag, and then we'll take you to Headquarters."

"How long do you think I'll be away?"

"I'm not sure at the moment. I'm not going to commit to one day or two days or a week, because the length is going to depend on our success in finding this android."

***

"Mathison. Come in, come in." John Eden stood up and beckoned. "Sergeant Stanton and Detective Heart of MetPol. They're investigating the death of Professor Delambre."

A bespectacled man in a lab coat walked over to the desk. "You mean the murder."

"Yes, yes. Come in." Eden pointed. "Bring a chair over."

Eden sat back down. "Officers, this is Mathison Clarke. He works in Artificial Intelligence and was a colleague of Delambre. They collaborated on various projects relating to the development of an artificial thought process."

"I said, 'Don't do this,'" Clarke said, "but they did it anyway. The idea itself was questionable, but to do a transfer from a brain that was already degraded? Foolish. Irresponsible."

"Did you work with Delambre and Bachmann?" Heart leaned forward, inquisitive.

"They consulted me but worked on their own."

"How often was Bachmann here?"

"A lot. I thought he and Delambre lived here at times."

"Did Bachmann ever talk about where he stayed?"

"You mean his home?" Clarke asked.

"That's across town. I was thinking of something closer by."

"I don't remember either one of them saying anything about that. However, on the occasions we've had people stay very late for meetings or seminars, we've put them up across the street at the Wyndham."

"The Wyndham Hotel," Heart said.

"Yes."

Heart sat with arms crossed, chin in hand. "Anything else, Mr. Clarke?"

"Yes. This android was an experimental model programmed with the latest in technology, offering interchangeability and auto-regen."

"Would you explain that?"

"Interchangeability means the android can swap parts. Take off a hand and put another in its place. Or a leg."

"Or a face."

"Yes," Clarke said. "We're looking at moving away from building fixed androids to allowing the customer to mix and match whatever parts they want to create one made to order."

"From what we've seen, it works all too well."

"Keep in mind, we never intended on having an android that thinks for itself. Delambre's experiment with Bachmann went way beyond anything we ever imagined."

"And the other thing you mentioned?"

"Auto-regen uses nanotechnology to repair damaged parts. Rather than coming back to us for service, an android could self-repair."

"That's another thing we can corroborate." Heart stood. "Sergeant, let's check the hotel. Gentlemen, thank you for your time."

***

"May we speak with your manager?" Stanton flashed her ID at the clerk manning the desk at the Wyndham Hotel.

"Down that hall. First door on your right."

Heart and Stanton entered the office, and she announced them. "Sergeant Stanton, Detective Heart, MetPol." She held out her ear-tab, set in hand-tab mode. The display showed her portrait with her insignia and the official MetPol logo. Heart stood to one side.

"Yes, ma'am, how can I help you?" The woman smiled, yet fidgeted.

"You are?"

"Joanna Loudon."

"I'm looking for somebody and you may be able to help." Stanton touched the display and the image of Willard Bachmann appeared. "Have you seen this man?"

"Yes."

"Have you seen him in the past twenty-four hours?"

"Oh, no. But he has stayed here during the past six months, sometimes up to a week at a time."

Stanton touched the display again to show the face of Patrick Klint. "This man?"

"He's been here, but I haven't seen him today. Although we do have several seminars in progress, and we're rather busy. I could have missed him."

"Would you search for the name Patrick Klint in your system?"

"Just a moment." Joanna touched the display on her desk. "I see we have two rooms registered under Patrick Klint: Room #217 and Room #1408."

"Are you sure?"

"See for yourself."

Stanton checked the monitor. "You have a service elevator?"

"Yes."

"I'd like you to take us up."

"Me?"

"Yes, you."

"But—"

"Now, Ms. Loudon. This is official police business."

They walked out into the bustling lobby without another word, but Stanton stopped short when she saw Charlie Vance walk from a bank of elevators and out the auto-slide front doors. Only then did she follow Heart and Joanna.

Stanton touched her ear-tab. "Team Leader?"

Joanna turned down a short hall. A nearby door marked Garage opened and the SWAT team filed in. Joanna thumbed a pad to open the elevator. Stanton waved everybody in before getting on herself. "Room #217, everybody."

A few seconds later, the doors opened at the end of a carpeted hallway. Joanna pointed. "Down that way, eighth door on the right."

"Stay here, and keep the doors open," Stanton said. "Team Leader, prepare the door."

The SWAT members rushed to the room, waiting as the leader worked with the panel. "Entry in three, two, one, go." All rushed in at once. A couple in their underwear was propped up in bed, watching a wall display. Two members pointed their weapons at them, shouting. "Don't move!" The man, having just bitten down on a croissant, froze. The woman gawked, eyes bulging.

A voice came from the bathroom. "Clear!"

Another member combed through the sitting area and riffled behind the curtains. "Clear!"

"I don't think this is our man," Heart said.

"Everybody out," Stanton said, watching as the squad filed out. Looking back, she said, "Sorry" and pulled the door shut.

The task force proceeded to the fourteenth floor.

"I'm expecting this to be it," Heart said, pulling his gun out of his shoulder holster.

"Entry in three, two, one, go."

The room was empty but for two suitcases. The first contained clothes, shoes, and other personal items. The second held android parts, divided into sections containing faces and hands. Heart looked at a slot labeled WB. He pulled out a face and held it up for Stanton. "Willard Bachmann." Putting the face back, he noted a section labeled PK and held up its contents. "Patrick Klint." He touched another section. "Curious. There's a third slot for CV, but it's empty."

"What?" Stanton leaned over to look, alarmed. "I just watched Charlie Vance get off the elevators and walk out. I avoided him due to your history. That was our man. Our guy is currently disguised as Vance!"

"Is he going to kill Ashaki Okafor?"

"She was next on the list. Do you think the arti-Bachmann is continuing with his original plan?"

Heart took out the communicator and pressed Call. "Come on, come on." There was a click.

"Voynich."

Heart's ear-tab showed the chief sitting at his desk. "We found our guy at the Wyndham Hotel, but we've missed him by minutes. We think he's disguised himself as Charlie Vance, and we think he's going to kill Ashaki Okafor."

"Okafor, along with Enapay, is attending a plenary meeting of the OligCouncil in one hour. The three missing members — Bachmann, Singh, and Rupert — will be represented by their seconds-in-command. The Outer Party will be there in full force, with every satrap in the city in attendance. If your man is going to do something drastic, this would seem like the perfect opportunity to get everybody at once."

"Would he know about the event?"

"You tell me. You've reported he knows what Bachmann knew and that he's plugged into everything going on, including email and personal communications. With his military connections and his access to equipment, who knows what or who he's spying on?"

Voynich leaned forward and touched something out of view. "Just a moment, Heart."

The audio muted and Heart watched the chief speak into a handheld device.

"What's the matter?" Stanton asked.

"Voynich is taking another call."

"We'll need help."

"He'll give it to us. This is too important."

The volume was restored.

"Heart?" Voynich put down the handheld.

"Yes, sir?"

"That was Marie Amble."

"Really?"

"She claims to have new information about Willard Bachmann."

"What'd she say?" Heart asked.

"She wants to talk in private."

"Why in private?"

"She's worried about spies. She's worried Bachmann may be intercepting her calls."

Heart nodded. "She's not the only one."

"There'll be a thousand people at this plenary session. I'm going to ramp up security, and I'm sending over a squad to back you up. But if you say your guy can change appearances, do you know if he'll remain as Charlie Vance? Couldn't he change into somebody else?"

"We saw indications of only three faces in the hotel room — two of which are still here."

"Still, we don't know if he has other hiding places," Voynich said. "There's no telling what other resources he may have at his disposal. I want you and your team to get to this meeting, find Charlie Vance, and place him in custody. At least we'll know it's not him if another Charlie Vance shows up."

"Yes, sir," Heart said.

"I'll go see Marie Amble and meet you at the session. Voynich out."

Chapter 15

"Team, I want one man at each entrance." Stanton pointed to various positions around the auditorium. "Take several guards with you. Distribute pictures of the suspect and verify every single person who shows up. You know our guy. Heart and I will survey the crowd."

Heart paced down a side aisle toward the platform at the front of the room. Stanton followed. He pressed his ear-tab and cast his viewer over the crowd. "Scan. Vance, Charles."

Some early arrivals were milling about, others sitting. There was the loud drone of conversation.

"I can't ID everybody." Heart moved toward the center. "Are you scanning, Stanton?"

"Yes."

Heart turned his head to the right and back to center. A man was bent over, fiddling with a briefcase. "There! I think that's him!" He pointed. "Twenty rows up, second seat in."

Heart bounded up the center aisle, pushing several people aside. Withdrawing his gun, Heart pointed it at the man's face. "Don't move!"

The man flung his hands up and shrank back in his seat. "Shit!"

"Who are you?" Heart demanded.

"J-J-J-Julius... Kelp." The man squirmed. "God, don't shoot me."

"Oh, crap," Heart said, holstering his gun. He took off his ear-tab and held it out. "Police. Look straight ahead for a retinal scan."

Kelp lowered his hands and leaned forward as Heart put the ear-tab back on. "Verify." He touched the ear-tab again. "Shit!"

Turning around, he came face-to-face with Stanton. "Not him."

"I noticed," she said as they walked back down the aisle.

"A thousand people. How are we supposed to find him in this crowd?" Heart scowled as he glanced over the room.

"What do you think Bachmann intends to do?"

"Your guess is as good as mine. Kill the last members of the oligarchy?"

"I don't see how that could do him any good. Command falls to the next in line, and one of the satraps steps up."

"He's got connections to the military. Could he be planning a coup?"

Stanton stopped and held his arm. "Wait. What?"

"Bachmann wants to take over, so he starts by killing members of the oligarchy. That destabilizes the council. Next up? A strongman takeover."

"The only way that would work is if the military backed him, and I don't see that happening. Would local police really go along with such a change of leadership? I can't see it."

They stopped in front of the stage and gazed over the crowd. A few stragglers came in from the side entrances, making their way to the last empty seats at the back.

Heart placed a foot on the first step of the dais. "Now what do we do?"

Stanton shrugged, helpless.

"Holy crap!" In the wings, Heart could see Chief Voynich and Charlie Vance standing face-to-face in conversation.

Heart bounded up the three steps onto the platform, Stanton directly behind. Dashing into the wing, he unholstered his gun, thrusting the muzzle into Vance's face. "Don't move!"

Vance stared at the end of the gun. "What—"

"Don't move, goddammit. I'll blow your head off." Heart touched his ear-tab. "Heat signature."

Stanton grabbed Voynich by the arms and moved him back. "Please, sir, step back." She stood in front of the chief, pointing her gun at Vance.

"What are you doing?" Voynich asked, perplexed.

"Look straight ahead." Heart took off his ear-tab and held it in front of Vance. "Retinal scan."

Vance moved his head. "What?"

Heart holstered his gun and seized Vance by the chin. "Don't move!" He held his ear-tab to the left eye. "Scan."

He put the ear-tab back on. "Verify," he said, pulling out his gun and pointing it at Vance's chest. His face fell.

"What's wrong?" Stanton asked.

Heart lowered his gun. "He checks out. He's human. That's Charlie Vance."

"Who else would I be, Matty?" Vance grinned.

"Shaddup."

"I have a speech to deliver, Officers." Voynich motioned to the podium. "If we're all clear here, let me begin."

Heart turned to Voynich as he holstered his gun. "You knew it was Vance."

"Yes, I did."

"How?"

"I know Mr. Vance."

"Could he have fooled you?"

"Officers aren't the only ones who can verify identities."

Heart stared at the chief, perplexed. "I suppose."

"Why don't all of you take your places and we can get started."

"You're speaking?"

"Yes. I'm addressing the plenary session."

"Oh." Heart gave Voynich a sidelong glance as the chief strode to center stage and stood behind the podium.

"I'll just take my seat," Vance said.

Heart grabbed him by the arm. "You'll be sitting with us." He led Vance down the steps to the reserved seating in front, placing Vance between himself and Stanton.

"Ladies and gentlemen." Voynich surveyed the room as people stopped talking and turned to listen.

"The OligCouncil has lost three of its five members: Willard Bachmann, Dhatri Singh, and Keith Rupert. Chapter four, paragraph six of the Metrofloat New York charter defines a quorum for the council as three. It goes on to explain that if a quorum cannot be convened, the power of the council falls to the chief of police."

Heart and Stanton looked at one another.

"At oh eight hundred today, I signed proclamation number

ten eighty-one, placing the entire city under martial law. The privilege of habeas corpus is suspended. All police, military, and support services will report to me. The OligCouncil is disbanded, effective immediately."

The room gave a collective gasp. People began murmuring to their neighbors.

Charlie Vance stood up and yelled. "You can't do that!"

"Sit down, Mr. Vance." Voynich pointed at his seat. "You're out of order."

Soon, other voices throughout the room were raised. "Unconstitutional!" "Unlawful!"

"What about our agreement?" Vance insisted.

Heart frowned, looking between Vance and Voynich.

"Sit down," Voynich said.

"You promised to make me a member of the council."

"Shut up!" Voynich pounded on the podium.

Several voices from the back yelled out. "Boo!"

Heart glanced back at the room, unsure what to make of this sudden turn of events.

"You can't do this, Bachmann." Vance shook his fist.

Heart and Stanton didn't have time to register these words before Voynich reached into his coat and pulled out a gun. Aiming the weapon at Vance, he calmly said, "Incendiary" and pulled the trigger.

Vance jerked and looked down at his stomach. He lurched forward, screaming as vapor and smoke rose from his midsection. He stumbled, falling onto the platform steps, before rolling onto his back and flailing his arms and legs. His abdomen turned into a single white flame.

The auditorium erupted in chaos: people yelled, jumped up out of their seats, and scrambled for the exits. Pulling out their weapons, Heart and Stanton moved toward the dais.

"Don't try it," Voynich said, turning his gun on them.

They froze.

"It's for your own good. It's for the good of everyone. I, and I alone, can control the council. I'll make things right — for all of us." Voynich aimed at the floor. "Smoke."

Heart and Stanton dove in opposite directions as a dull bang sounded and smoke billowed, forming a blinding fog. Heart coughed, scrambling to one side and running back onto the dais. But he was now aiming at an empty podium.

"Where'd he go?" Heart yelled.

"I see nothing on the scan!" Stanton called back.

"CV... That didn't mean Charlie Vance. It meant Chief Voynich."

"He must've been with Marie Amble."

"Has he killed the chief? We need to get there ASAP! I hope Amble can give us an idea of what Bachmann is up to."

"To the car! Quick!"

Pushing past the panicking crowd, Stanton and Heart ran out of the auditorium toward the parking area. The got into their flivver. It had just exited the building and pulled into the main traffic corridor at the twentieth level when they heard a dull thud. The car stopped and spun around. They spied Voynich, standing through the sunroof of a flivver stationed by the opposite building. Putting down a hand gun, he lifted a launcher onto his shoulder.

"Drop! Drop!" Heart yelled.

Stanton cut the AG and the flivver plummeted. There was an explosion as the vehicle twisted sideways, hurtling into the side of a building and creating a shower of splintered glass. The car tipped, now pointing straight down. Heart felt weightless and glanced at the altimeter. They had less than three seconds before they hit ground. He steadied himself between the console and the dashboard as story after story swept by in a blur.

Stanton hit the AG and the flivver rapidly decelerated, slamming them back into their seats. The car's left side hit the abutment of a building and flipped over. Upside down, the officers flopped around as they crashed into a parked vehicle and skidded into a pedestrian mall. People screamed and scattered.

Hanging upside down by their safety belts, Heart and Stanton listened to the pinging of debris as it rained down on the undercarriage of their car. They twisted to look at each other.

"Holy crap!" Heart said. "That was close."

There was a loud thump behind the flivver and the vehicle shook.

"Did Bachmann blow off a section of the building?" he asked.

"Let's get out of here," Stanton said.

Heart twisted, placing a foot on the dashboard and untying his safety belt before easing himself onto the roof. The door wouldn't open. Holding the back of his seat, he raised both legs and kicked. The metal groaned as he kicked again. Finally, the door gave way and he crawled out.

Stanton had climbed out her side and was surveying the car.

"I'd call it a write-off," Heart said.

"We need another car, right away." Stanton scanned the area and then strode over to a flivver and touched the door. "MetPol override security clearance authorization Alfa Alfa three-zero-five." The door opened.

"That's a good trick," Heart said. "I really must learn it." Grinning, he climbed into the passenger seat.

Stanton touched the dashboard. "Safe House Kilo Alfa four-six-zero." The car rose into the air. "Call Central. Request backup at the safe house. Priority One. Suspect has kidnapped, and may have killed, Chief Voynich."

"Bachmann's got to know he can't get away with this," Heart said.

"Amble said he wasn't thinking normally. Maybe psychosis is part of his condition?"

"He's unpredictable. He's also determined." Heart stared at the passing buildings. "This isn't going to end well."

***

The car circled the building at the tenth level as the officers looked through the windows of the safe house.

"No flivver," Stanton said.

"That doesn't mean he isn't already here, with the car parked elsewhere." Heart pointed. "Go to the south entrance."

"I've signaled clearance to the security perimeter." Stanton watched out the window as the car docked itself. Opening her door, she stepped into the entrance. Heart was right behind.

Stanton walked to a wall panel, holding her index finger to the touch pad. "I'm connecting to the security system and scanning all rooms." She glanced at Heart. "It's registering two people. The ID chips show Marie Amble and Chief Voynich. They're both alive."

"That's promising. What about Bachmann?"

"The system shows no one else."

"Could Bachmann override the system?"

"He's resourceful, so I wouldn't be surprised if he could."

"Where are they?"

"In the living room."

"Let's start there."

Unholstering their guns, they tiptoed down the hall and peeked through a door. Marie Amble and Chief Voynich were sitting on couches across from one another, separated by a low glass table. Voynich's head was tilted to one side, eyes shut.

Stanton and Heart scanned the room but could see no one else there.

Nodding to each other, they stepped through the door, sweeping the area with their weapons. Amble turned to them but said nothing. Heart followed her line of sight and then whipped around and fired. Yet his weapon did not discharge.

"I've disabled your guns." Bachmann appeared in the doorway. "You might as well put them away. They're no good here."

Stanton and Heart fiddled with the mechanisms as they glanced at each other, begrudgingly holstering their weapons.

Bachmann strode into the room. "Now that we're all together..."

There was a hiss as a sliding panel closed the open door.

"Safe rooms in a safe house. Why not?" Bachmann walked to the window and turned to face the room at large.

Heart was leaning over Voynich. "What's the matter with him?"

"Incapacitated. Drugged. I couldn't have him alert the authorities while I was masquerading as the chief of police."

"You didn't kill him?"

"I'm going to harvest his brain. I'm sure there is valuable information locked away in his memories."

"What's the point of all this? What's the goal?"

"Power, Detective Heart. Power over everything. Democracy is such a slow process, and I'm in a hurry."

Heart stepped toward one side of the room and leaned against a serving table. "Power corrupts."

"Yes, yes. And absolute power blah, blah, blah. An aphorism from weak people without vision. Unfortunately, democracy gives power to small-minded, uninformed voters who are only motivated by self-interest. They can't see the bigger picture. They hold back the true visionaries. The biggest obstacle to progress is inertia, and the masses want to remain as they are. They abhor change, and so, change must be thrust upon them."

Heart glanced at Stanton, who was sneaking around the opposite side of the room. "So you're the visionary. You're the one to lead us out of the wilderness?"

"It sounds poetic but, yes, I'm the one. There's a lot to be said for a benevolent dictatorship."

"Are you benevolent, Bachmann?"

"I'm thinking of the greater good. The OligCouncil was a democracy with all its faults: the infighting, the backstabbing, the maneuvering for a better position. It was all a distraction from the bigger goal of getting everyone to move in the same direction at the same time."

Heart picked up a water glass as Bachmann pointed the gun at him. "Don't be foolish, Detective Heart."

Remaining calm, Heart looked at the gun and then picked up a pitcher and poured water into the glass. He took a sip.

"By supplanting the council, I remove the last obstacle to my vision of the future. It's an exciting time."

"You'll never get away with this," Heart said.

"Oh, but I am getting away with it. Your call for backup will go unheeded. I've changed the coordinates of this safe house in the system and, as we speak, your forces are off to another address in the wrong section of town. By the time they figure out the issue, we'll be finished our business, and I'll be ensconced in my new position as the de facto head of Metrofloat New York."

Raising his hand, Heart rubbed his temple in a slow, deliberate movement. He threw the glass at Bachmann as Stanton ran in from the other side and grabbed Bachmann's wrist and gun. Twisting them upwards, she pivoted and threw the man over her shoulder. He fell through the glass table with a loud crash. She wrenched at the firearm, but he held fast and fired. The bullet smashed through a window.

Bachmann rolled over and got up on his knees. Stanton kicked at him, still yanking the gun left and right. He grasped her leg, knocking her off balance. She fell to the floor, landing hard on her back.

Heart grabbed the water pitcher and smashed it on top of Bachmann's head. "Goddamn you!"

Bringing his other hand to the firearm, Bachmann continued to struggle against Stanton's grip as Heart pounded on Bachmann's back. With a sudden lurch, Bachmann shifted his weight toward Stanton and forced the weapon's muzzle in her direction. "Incendiary."

Heart kicked Bachmann as he fired and Stanton's chest exploded in flames.

"No!" Heart yelled, immobilized. Bachmann scooted backward, scrambling to his feet.

Stanton's body spasmed several times and was still.

Picking up a steel floor lamp, Heart swung it, hard. The base caught Bachmann on the left side of his head with a resounding thunk, sparks jumping out of a large gash. Bachmann rushed Heart and seized him by the throat, lifting him off the floor, before throwing him across the room. "I will not be thwarted." Heart slammed into the opposite wall, where he collapsed to the floor. He moaned in pain.

"Willard!" Amble now stood, hands on her hips. "When is it going to stop?"

"But they're against me. They want to prevent me from reaching my goal."

"Willard, do you love me?"

"Of course I do."

"Do you trust me?" Amble asked.

"Yes... to a point."

"Would the man I love do this? Kill people? Subvert the council? Would he make himself dictator?"

"But—"

"But what? This isn't right. You're not right. This is crazy. You're crazy." Anger filled Amble's voice.

"Be careful, Marie."

"Be careful? Are you going to kill me too, Willard? When is it going to stop? How many people are you going to kill before you realize this isn't working? You can't force your way to the top. You'll end up having to kill everybody to do that."

"Shut up, Marie."

Heart stumbled to his feet.

"So you don't love me," Amble said.

"I do love you."

"But you're going to kill me."

"You're preventing me from reaching my goal."

"It's an evil goal."

"You're trying to stop me like they're trying to stop me." Bachmann had raised his gun and was pointing it at Amble.

Heart stepped closer, desperately trying to assess the situation.

"Go ahead, Willard," Amble said. "Go ahead and kill the woman you say you love. How do you explain that contradiction?"

"You're confusing me, Marie." Bachmann glanced at Heart as he took another step forward. "I'll deal with you in a moment."

Taking out his gun, Heart aimed it at Bachmann's head.

"MetPol override security clearance authorization Alfa Alfa three-zero-five. Explosive." He squeezed the trigger several times, but nothing happened.

Distracted, Bachmann shoved Heart, who fell backward and lay sprawled on the floor. "Do you think I hadn't covered that possibility?" he sneered.

Bachmann turned back to Amble. "Marie, I want you to understand."

Again, Heart staggered to his feet and took aim. "MetPol override security clearance authorization Kilo Alfa four-six-zero-one-seven-zero-four. Explosive."

There was an audible click, and Bachmann whipped around. "Oh sh—"

Heart fired.

A hole appeared between Bachmann's eyes, and a thump sounded from inside his head. Puffs of smoke blew out his ears and his eyes popped out, hanging against his cheeks by metallic filaments. The body teetered and toppled over.

Heart gawked at his gun. "I had no idea that would work."

Twisting around, he holstered the weapon and rushed over to Stanton. "Shit! Shit! Shit!" Panic-stricken, he stared at the gaping hole in her chest and shook his fists as he paced around the body. "Oh my God!" He gasped as his voice broke. Grabbing both his temples, Heart let out a groan. "Oh, Elizabeth. I'm so, so sorry."

He knelt and felt around the opening in her chest, examining the internal mechanisms. After a few moments, Heart leaned back on his heels and let out a long sigh. "Damn. We had just met." He shook his head. "I was looking forward to getting to know you better."

Heart looked around the room. Amble sat on the couch, staring at Willard's body. She seemed to be in a state of shock. Voynich remained unconscious.

He heard a beep of an incoming call. Frowning, he touched his ear-tab. "Hello?"

"Are you going to get maudlin on me, Heart?"

"Who's this?"

"Stanton."

Heart looked down at her face. Her mouth was still, but her eyes turned to him. He jerked back, startled. "Whoa! Is this a joke?"

"No, I'm here. I'm still functioning."

"I don't understand."

"The blast simply shut down my body. My brain survives thanks to emergency backup. I can't move, but I'm alive. However, I'm going to need serious repair work to get my systems back up and running."

"You can hear me."

"Yes."

"You can see me."

"Yes."

"But you can't talk?"

"No, talking's part of my body functions, and all that is currently off line. I can see and hear, but I'm mute. Fortunately, I have a short-range radio connection, so I can contact you and still communicate. It's also part of my emergency systems."

"You're down but not out." Heart grinned.

"Call for backup. Not having a body isn't fun."

Epilogue

Heart emptied a drawer, stuffing the contents into a kit bag.

"Will I ever see you again?" Sally sat on the bed, tears brimming in her eyes.

He smiled. "It's not like I'm that far away."

"People in the city never come here to visit. They never see us grounders."

"I'll be back," he said, crouching in front of her and taking her hands. "I promise to come see you, but there's something else I want."

"What?"

"I want you to come visit me."

Sally's eyes widened. "In the city?"

"Yes."

"I've never been to the city." She grinned. "What's it like? I've heard it has a million lights. With tall buildings. And clean streets."

"It has all of those things. And more."

"More?"

"Restaurants, stores, museums, parks. There are lots of things to do."

Sally clapped her hands. "Oh, goodie!"

Heart slung his bag over his shoulder and took Sally's hand. "Walk me down to the taxi."

They strolled down the hall to the front of the Low Cost Lodge as an autocab swooped in and settled on the ground. He opened the side door and tossed his bag across the seat.

"You can call me anytime."

Sally held her arms up, and he pulled her into a tight hug. She kissed his cheek. "Bye, Matty. I'll miss you."

He stood and looked at the motel that had been his home for five years of his life. Could he pick up his career where it had left off?

Sally sniffed.

"Are you crying?"

"No."

"Yes, you are," he said, crouching back down and wiping her cheek with a finger. "I'm only a call away."

"But you're not going to be down the hall."

"True. But, what about you and your mom? You're moving in a month, too. You're not going to be here either."

She wiped her nose on the back of her hand. "Is she going to say yes to him?"

"She already did, but she wants to transition first. You're going to have a dad."

"He's nice to me."

Heart kissed her cheek. "Goodbye, Sally. No, not goodbye. See you soon!" He grinned.

She grinned back at last. "So long, Matty. Catch some crooks!"

He climbed into the taxi, and, as it rose, he continued to wave at Sally. She was looking up at the cab, both arms raised and gesturing wildly with her hands.

***

"Voynich has fully recovered and reconvened the council," Cranston said. "Rights of succession have satraps taking over, and so the five oligarchs continue. It's business as usual."

"A happy ending." Heart sipped his artihol. "Although, I was convinced that wouldn't be the case." He looked at Stanton.

Cranston nodded and turned to her. "Speaking of which, what did you feel, exactly? You suffered a complete system shutdown."

"I didn't feel anything." Stanton eyed her glass as she turned it around. "The sensors cut off, and there was no feedback. It's like when you sleep on your arm and cut off the blood supply. You can't feel it or move it."

"But you were conscious the whole time."

"I could see and hear, but I couldn't move. I could only talk through comms. It was strange."

"Thank God for backup systems."

"Yeah." She held up her empty glass. "Anybody want another?"

"I won't say no," Heart said.

Stanton waved toward the bar to no effect. "Everybody's busy," she said, standing. "I'll be right back."

Cranston and Heart watched her walk off.

"You two make a good team."

Heart took a sip. "I guess so."

"I've known Elizabeth for some time."

"Yes."

"I can read her."

"Read what?" Heart frowned.

"There's something there," Cranston said.

"What do you mean?"

"She's fond of you."

"We're partners."

"There's more. She's been through a lot, and she's pushed away her old self. But she's fond of you." Cranston glanced over Heart's head and smiled.

"She's a tough woman," Heart said.

"But she's different."

"You mean because she's a synth?"

"Yes."

Heart leaned back in his chair. "That's just a label. Whether she's whole, a synth, or a mixture with prosths, none of that matters." He raised his left hand and touched his temple with his index finger. "It's what's up here that counts. She's a human being. She's a woman."

Something seized his wrist and lifted him out of his seat. Heart dangled over his chair until he twisted around to find himself looking into Stanton's eyes. She had braced herself against the railing of the upper level. Cranston laughed in the background.

"What are you doing?" Heart exclaimed.

She leaned closer and put her face to his. "Shut up and kiss me."

Acknowledgements

My thanks to the following people for their editorial assistance:

rmburgess
Jennifer Dinsmore
Kit Duncan
Sherry Hinman
Heather Kohlmann
Vanessa Wells

I also thank the beta readers for their invaluable input.

About the Author

William Quincy Belle is just a guy. Nobody famous; nobody rich; just some guy who likes to periodically add his two cents worth with the hope, accounting for inflation, that $0.02 is not over evaluating his contribution. He claims that at the heart of the writing process is some sort of (psychotic) urge to put it down on paper and likes to recite the following, which so far he hasn't been able to attribute to anyone: "A writer is an egomaniac with low self-esteem." You will find Mr. Belle's unbridled stream of consciousness floating around in cyberspace.

Life, Love & the Big D
Ten Short Stories about How Things Work Out
We're born. We die. We marry. We divorce. Here are ten short stories about how things work out. Sometimes it's good, and sometimes it's bad. However, no matter what the results are, no matter the pain and anguish we all live through or the happiness we find, this is our life. As a wise man once said, "If you hang in there long enough, you'll grow old and die."

Why Fi: Vol. 1
Five Short Stories of Speculative Fiction
Why (sci-)fi: because it's fun to think about what doesn't (yet) exist.

Science fiction or speculative fiction? Here are short stories speculating about the future when science has figured it all out: outer space, inner space, rocket ships, teleportation, alternate worlds and alternate realities. The future looks interesting, even exciting, but it's not without its dangers.

Why Fi: Vol. 2
Ten More Short Stories of Speculative Fiction
Further musings about the future and science.

Salmagundi
Twelve Short Stories: A Hodgepodge of the Heinous, Horrifying, and Humorous
salmagundi (noun) – a mixed dish
Recipe: Take the heinous — crime as a mixture of robbery and murder — and blend in the horrifying — monsters both real and sadistic — then sprinkle with humor — a chuckle and the occasional guffaw. Serve liberally with a gasp and a smile. Enjoy. Low in calories, no cholesterol, and contributes to the health of your (funny) bone: key to a good sense of humerus.

Death is a Many-Splendored Thing
Fourteen Short Stories About Our Final Exit
We all die. Rich, poor, famous, unknown, cultured, or uneducated, we all leave this world. Some of us leave naturally, some of us leave accidentally, and some of us leave deliberately. Yet no matter what any of us do, we all face that final moment of our lives.

Author's Note
These stories are based on real life: news articles, random things from the Internet, and personal accounts given to me by family and friends. Horror is not necessarily monsters and crazed serial killers, but rather our day-to-day lives and the sometimes overwhelming difficulties we face.

Connect with William Quincy Belle

Like my book? Tell your friends. Didn't like it? Please don't firebomb my house.

Visit me on my web site:
http://www.williamquincybelle.com

Friend me on Facebook:
https://www.facebook.com/WilliamQuincyBelle

Follow me on Twitter:
https://twitter.com/wqbelle

Stalk me on Google.
https://www.google.com

Made in the USA
Middletown, DE
05 March 2019